MW01110287

The Project

Theme: Beginnings

Editors

Sean Froyd
Keith Johnson
Joshua Page

Proofreader
Sharon Simpson

Table of Contents

Forward

First things first, thank you for purchasing a copy of <u>The Project</u>, a new magazine devoted to being free from the boundaries of genre. The idea came to Mr. Froyd and me while sitting at the local pub, which is a place where many good ideas briefly come to life but rarely see the light of the next morning. After a few pints and a bit of discussion about the merits and flaws of online publishing, we ended up talking about the creative writing journals that he had worked on in college. I can't remember now how we made that leap but the concept was out there, one that he was interested in pursuing again without the restrictions of the college system, one that we had full control over and could publish what we wanted the way we wanted. This sparked my interest since I've always been a fan of science-fiction and fantasy magazines and short story collections. The problem that we ran into was that there are so many magazines already on the market covering every imaginable genre, there was a magazine for any taste and any niche we chose would already be filled. Why choose one genre and limit ourselves when we can use them all? That was the idea, toss labels out the window and just publish good stories. Why does it matter if it's science-fiction or a mystery? A good story is a good story and no label should, or can, take that away.

To make it interesting, we came up with the concept of basing each issue on a theme, a central idea that we could use to focus the writings and pull the whole thing together. Our first theme of

"Beginnings" wasn't as obvious as it sounds. We started with things like birth or invention but it occurred to us that making the theme too specific would constrict certain writers. It's all well and good to have invention as a theme if you are targeting science-fiction writers; but what would non-fiction writers do? We solved this by broadening the theme, and since all of our ideas focused on a start of some kind we decided on "Beginnings".

Creating the magazine was a fun experience, but it was also a learning experience. Being an editor turned out to be more difficult than I thought it would be. It's easy to say you like a story or dislike it but hard to explain why. Sometimes it can be as obvious as awkward grammar or a disjointed plot but other times it's simply a feeling that something isn't right. When words failed me to explain these feelings about stories to my fellow editors, I realized how much easier it is to be a critic than an editor. Pointing out a story's flaws is one thing, but telling them how to fix them is quite another matter. I hope as this journey continues I become better at it, better at pinpointing the various bits and pieces that don't work and finding the solutions to fix them.

In the mean time, please enjoy the stories we have found for you in our first issue. Every story deserves to be told and we are glad you are taking the time to give these a chance. This is why we publish, to give stories a chance to be told so they can enlighten, inspire or maybe just make us smile.

Keith M Johnson

Reactionaries
By Josh Almendinger

Josh Almendinger lives in northern Minnesota with his loving wife and a spoiled dachshund. He wiles away his hours reading, playing games of all kinds, and imagining worlds for his friends to adventure in. When not engaged in these activities he writes imaginative fiction like this wonderful piece, "Reactionaries", which we hope he continues for future issues.

      Jules woke with a start. The pungent odors of sweat, sex, and perfume mingled in the stale air of the prostitute's room in which he had awakened. He rose quietly from the tussled mattress on which the courtesan still slumbered peacefully, feeling a familiar pull in the back of his mind. He was being called to duty. Pinpricks of light made their way through the shuttered windows, scattered against and flickered upon his naked body as he made his way across the room to his clothing. He dressed hastily and strapped on his belt and holster. A massive revolver now hung at his hip. A brief memory of riding with the United States Dragoons returned to him. He recalled the day he was issued the revolver, thinking it a ridiculous and cumbersome weapon, it had since saved him more times than he cared to count. Even now, he carried it as a last resort. He pulled on his long, blue overcoat. Numerous strips of differently colored cloth were sewn delicately onto it and they seemed to flutter in an unseen wind as he donned it. He slung his rifle over his shoulder, and stepped out into the hallway. The whore let out a mewling sigh and rolled over in her sleep.

The hall was dimly lit, the light from the gas lanterns lining the wall flickered off the polished hardwood floors of the Coy Coquette, one of Folkhill's cleaner operating brothels. Jules found solace in its accidental likeness to the bars and bawdy houses of the Prime's American Old West. Something lay on the floor before him. Something so dark that it seemed as though it was absorbing the scant light of the hallway, pulling it into itself and becoming all the darker for it. Jules bent down and picked it up with a smile. It was a hat made of some kind of dark felt, likely woven in one of the Shadow planes. But this... this was not just any hat. This was that sap, Lyre's hat. This was already shaping up to be an interesting day indeed.

Jules strode out into the bustling street, taking in the sounds and scents of the City of Pleasures before taking his second step onto the Celestial Highway and out of this plane of existence. He vanished before the eyes of the peddlers and street-walkers that surrounded him who seemed none-too-surprised.

The Highway stretched out before and behind him and on either side, the amalgam of everything that is, was, and ever will or could be. Jules slung his shoulder pack before him and began rummaging around inside until he pulled from it a scroll, neatly tied with a scarlet ribbon. Opening it, he read:

From the office of Darhmak,
RE: Assignment 433907
Bearer: Jules Brokentide
The Sending of Beryll Sivultem is hereby
requested. Subject last seen in the Barrow
Flats, in the Plane of Seminal
Contemplation. Considered Reactionary and
dangerous.

P.S.
Best of luck.

Jules had read so many of these that he scarcely saw anything in them other than the name and location of the subject. But this one was different. Reactionary? The term used for a soul that was highly adaptable and bore the ability to change its form upon a whim. Some were dangerous and tenacious and often turned on the Bearer of Burden charged with their sending, often killing the fresh ones. Others were elusive and extremely difficult to track down and locate. Either way, this was going to be a challenge. Jules cracked a grin. How long had it been since he had had such an assignment? And what was with that post script? "Best of Luck?" That was certainly out of the ordinary for HQ. The damnable bureaucrats didn't give a toss about their agents, much less Jules himself. The sentiment went unappreciated by this Bearer of Burden.

Jules shoved the missive back into his satchel and looked up, searching for the proper crossroad which would take him on the path to the Plane of Seminal Contemplation, and saw a figure fast approaching. Bathed in the bright light of the infinite cosmos at the man's back, his face was cloaked in shadows until the two were within spitting distance of each other. As Jules' eyes adjusted to the contrast of light and shadow he came to recognize the wanderer as Lyre, a fellow Bearer of Burden and the true owner of the hat which he now wore. Lyre raised his hand in greeting and Jules rolled his eyes. It wasn't that Jules had anything in particular against this man, he just 'didn't like the cut of his jib,' as they say. He was, what Jules named, a Passion Hunter. One whose only joy in life came from the completion of his missions. Never one for women or drink, it was especially grand to have found his hat lying on the floor of a whore house not five planes back.

"What's the good word, Jules?" Lyre chimed as they neared one another.

"I've not a single one for you, Lyre." Jules kept up his rapid gait.

"Say... Where'd you get that hat, partner?" Lyre asked, a quizzical tone in his voice.

"Ah! Now that you mention it, I can't quite recall in which specific Plane or Verse I happened upon it. Hmm... Try as I might I just can't seem to conjure an answer for you! Please, ask when next we meet, perhaps by then I may have remembered." Jules grinned. Better to play it stupid for now and walk on by. He didn't have time to inquire as to what exactly Lyre's hat was doing in the Coy, or to rub it in.

"Yeah, I guess I'll do just that then, huh?" Lyre said to Jules' back as they both continued on their respective ways.

Jules reached the road to Seminal Contemplation and took it. He took a glass vial, its cork sealed in a green wax, from his pouch and held it up to the light. An opaque, silvery liquid swished about in the vial, sometimes appearing to move with Jules' own motions and sometimes appearing to move of its own accord. Jules frowned and placed the container back inside his pouch. It would just have to be enough. He stepped off the Celestial Highway and into an arid and hilly land. The wind howled with the fury of a banshee, setting the swatches of colored cloth on Jules' coat awhirl, but stirring not the hat upon his head. Delighted, Jules stood atop a stone jutting from the peak of a hill, one of the thousands that made up the expanse, stretching out as far as the eye could see. Each and every one of them hollow and cold, housing the souls of infinite restless spirits foiled by their own introspective and paralyzing thoughts.

Jules bent down and once again produced the small vial of mysterious liquid. He cut through the wax with his thumbnail, uncorked it, and attempted to pour a small amount on the ground. At first, the fluid held to the bottom of the vial, quivering as if fighting gravity itself, not wanting to leave its snug and cozy home. But an instant later and it shot forth from the mouth of the vial and streaked off into the distance at the speed of light.

"Damn!" Jules muttered. He had only intended to use a drop, as the Quicksilver was valuable and hard to come by, even for a Bearer of Burden. Alas, the stuff had lived up to its name and was gone before he knew it, leaving a thin trail of silver behind to show where it had gone. Jules took his rifle from his shoulder and clipped the bayonet in place. Drawn to souls as restless and wild as itself, the Quicksilver would lead him to his quarry, and when he found it, he would send the soul exactly where it belonged, just as he had done so many times before. Jules began to run.

His legs carried him quickly, and seemed to possess the endurance of time and the elements themselves. There was no need to stoop and check the trail, the Quicksilver had left a mercurial trace of itself as it sped across the fells and knolls, bending and weaving its way toward a kindred spirit. As Jules crested a hill he spied what appeared to be a jagged black fingernail on the horizon. In the dim light that broke through the charcoal gray clouds above him, he traced the silver line which he followed. Stopping to catch his breath, he squinted at the thing on the horizon. A tower stood there, out of place in the hilly desolation that surrounded him. As he stared, surprised to find himself in wonderment, something flashed, golden atop the citadel. Curious, Jules sped on.

***

The din inside the tower was somehow comforting to Beryll Silvultem. The clatter of weights and the grinding of the massive gears and sprockets seemed to calm his racing mind. Although he could make little sense of the mechanisms that surrounded him, he assumed that they were all working happily in concert with each other to run the giant clock whose face beamed from atop the tower. It was dim inside, with dust motes dancing across the few rays of light that penetrated the gloom through holes in the walls and cracks in the crumbling mortar. It was loud, rhythmic, calm, and claustrophobic. To Beryll, it felt like home. No. Not home. Stockwood Sanitarium, the place he'd had no choice but to call home.

Less of a hospital and more of a house of horrors, escaping Stockwood had been no mean feat. When first he arrived, he had been confined to his "room" for no less than three weeks. The doctors believed that given his violent history, perhaps isolation would cure him. And isolation it was. The room was scarcely large enough for him to lay down upon the cold and filthy floor with his knees drawn up to his chest. He had sobbed himself to sleep every time he woke for the first couple of days. When finally he pulled himself together, he took stock of his surroundings. For as narrow a room as it was, it stood perhaps ten feet tall. A small hole adorned the wall at its ceiling where a brick was missing, replaced instead, with three thick iron bars. He was fed twice in all that time. A small slit would open up in the bottom of the door and a wooden bowl slid carelessly through, spilling its noxious contents upon the floor as the steel trap slammed shut behind it with a metallic 'clank.'

Sometimes, as the sun began to rise outside those walls, bats would fly in through the bars seeking refuge from the coming day and to rest before the night that followed. More than once, in desperate hunger, he had scaled the walls to snatch the small creatures and devour them whole, wincing as he forced himself to swallow the bones, fur, and all. The first he had tried to ration, eating only the top half before wrapping the rest in a small piece of his shirt to be saved for the next time the hunger was too painful to bear. When two more days passed without food, he unwrapped the precious leavings and gnawed slowly on what was left, only to vomit all that he had eaten onto the floor before him. He painfully continued to dry heave long after his stomach was empty. After that he decided that the only way to consume the wretched things was while they were fresh, while their blood was still warm.

When finally the door swung open, a great light blinded him. After a moment his eyes adjusted and a dark silhouette stepped in front of the light. Overcome with rage he leapt on the figure. Taking the doctor's head between his hands, he forced him to the floor. Two large men, one on either side of him, shouted, cursed, and tried with all their might to pull Beryll off the screaming doctor. Beryll held on with the unnatural strength that comes only to the most desperate of men. Groping, his thumbs happened on the doctor's eyes. With a horrific howl he forced his thumbs down through them, they popped like plums, a greasy mixture of viscous fluid and blood spurting forth from the empty sockets where the doctor's eyes used to be and onto Beryll's face. Undaunted he kept up the pressure until finally the doctor went limp and silent. Beryll smiled, the bloody mess oozing down his face and into his mouth. Licking his lips he began to laugh before he felt a sharp blow to the back of his head and the world went black again.

He woke with no knowledge of how long he had been out. He could make out the now familiar shapes of stones that made up his cramped cell through the gloom. Sharp, intense flashes of pain ignited his world as he tried to move from the suffocating ball his body was in. His knees were painfully jutting into his chest. His arms locked backwards and pressed to either side of him by what could only be a band of iron arching over his tiny frame. Each small movement produced an agonizing pain throughout his lungs and extremities as he tried to wiggle fee of the thick iron band compressing his body. He could feel the broken bones of his ribcage tearing into his lungs like ragged blades of fire.

Panic set in as each attempt managed only to amplify the intensity of his suffering. His breathing became erratic. Each time he exhaled he exhausted the air in his lungs, and each new breath he took was shallower than the last. Slowly he began to regain his composure, willing himself to breath slower and more rhythmically. He closed his eyes, and began to weep. His uncontrollable sobbing wracked his body with pain. The stabbing pain in his lungs and chest grew more and more violent with each sob, arcs of searing lightning played across his eyelids with each new jolt of pain. Opening them he was met with a view of the cold stone floor he had slept upon these countless nights, and the shocking realization that this would indeed be his last view of the friendless and harsh world that would end for him here.   Through a blur of tears, he spotted a small, black lump in his peripheral vision and recalled the bat he had captured before the door had opened and he exacted his vengeance upon the doctor. His sobs resumed and with futility he began to imagine himself as the bat. Free from the frigid stone and tall, constricting walls of his prison. Free from the agony of his body, and the loneliness of his mind. Free from the hopelessness wrought from the last few months locked away from the world. He closed his eyes.

He opened them and the pain was gone. The darkness around him had suddenly become a soft blue haze. He tried to stand. Fell. He threw his arms out before him to catch himself, and saw that they were wings. Black, leathery wings, with small claws extending from a joint half a wing's length from his torso. He turned and saw his crippled body, still locked firmly in the jaws of the scavenger's daughter. Somewhere inside he laughed. Taking flight with ease he reached the narrow, barred window, and flew off into the night.

Jules had lain prone beside a boulder at the crest of a hill with a clear view of the clock-tower, not a hundred and fifty yards before him. He peered through his scope, a dark cross hair scanning the sides of the tower and the giant, bronze face of the clock that adorned it just beneath its peak. He smirked as he recalled delicately drawing that cross hair with a quill stolen from the demon whose blood had served as the ink.   Performing the task had not been easy, but had bestowed the crystal lens with remarkable qualities. He need only desire the range he wished to view through it and blink. The scope would do the rest, granting him an unparalleled vision of his target, regardless of how far it lay. He had followed the quicksilver to the tower and saw that its slick trail ran up the side of the tower and into one of the many cracks that spider-webbed the surface of its walls. Between one of the fissures he spied movement. A large, dark shape was pacing just on the other side of the wall. Jules' smirk became a grin as he lined his cross hair up with the shadowy bulk through a hole in the mortar. He held his breath...

          A flash of silver near his clawed feet caught the corner of Beryll's eye. Looking down he saw what looked like the trail of a particularly wet slug near his feet. Bending down to examine it further, he heard a quiet crack off in the distance over the cacophony of grinding gears and squeaking pulleys. He yowled in pain and fury as a red blossom bloomed to fill the newly formed hole in his side. He stumbled in agony toward the open archway of a window to his right. He fell out of the portal and spread his wings, pumping them twice to steady himself in the air. Another crack in the distance, somewhere in front of him, and his right shoulder was hammered backwards throwing his flight off balance momentarily and causing him to fall a short span. The flesh around the wound sprang to life, twisting and reforming itself into tendrils stretching across the gaping hole to close it and stop the pulsing flow of blood. Not too far off in the distance he saw a glint of light near a boulder at the top of a small hill. Wheeling, he sped toward it.

Jules racked another round into the chamber, took aim at the renegade soul, and fired. The beast was huge, and not difficult to hit at this distance. Jules viewed the creature through his scope. Its great flat face twisted in pain, its mouth gaping to reveal rows of needle sharp teeth as it cried out. Its massive black wings beat slowly against the cool air as it quickly closed the distance between them. Jules worked deftly to load yet another enchanted cartridge, centered the cross hair over what he could only assume to be the creature's heart. He squeezed the trigger. The bullet hit home, blowing a large hole in the center of the chest of the soul. The beast's wings folded in around it as it fell from the sky. Jules began to run to where Beryll was falling, intent on finishing things up close. As he ran he saw long, fleshy, tentacles shoot out from the center mass of the wounded gargoyle and rapidly form a cocoon around it. As it hit the ground the tentacles pulled back into the monster revealing first the large head of a dog, followed then by massive legs that hit the ground running.

The mastiff growled as it rapidly closed the distance between them. Jules braced his rifle against his hip and leveled the blade of his bayonet at the charging hound. Jules let out a guttural war-cry as beast and man met in a flurry of blood, limbs, teeth and fur. Jules' bayonet struck home in the neck of the fiend. It bucked off to the side, the bayonet sliding from its muscles, the muscles themselves uncoiling from bone, probing, attempting to find a new way to mend their wounds. The brute rolled upon the ground, howling and spitting. Jules took the opportunity. He leapt into the air, gripping his rifle in two hands, and came down hard, feeling each bone of the mongrel's ribcage break as his bayonet pierced down and through, pinning it to the ground.

Panting, Jules turned to view the soul in its death throes. Instead, he watched with a growing sense of horror as narrow limbs broke through the skin and fur and the dog became a sort of amorphous blob of pulsating flesh and tendons. Eyeballs formed, disintegrated, and reformed as they seemingly floated across the surface of the formless ball of tissue and bone. The meat split, spitting out a large raven, feathers sopping with pus. No less than three hooked beaks protruded from the abomination's head as it flew straight and fast towards Jules' head. Without thinking he pulled his revolver from its holster and fired. The shot cleared the bird which morphed yet again within a split second of the bullet's impact, leaving behind a husk of tissue which fell behind it with a wet, plopping sound. Jules stepped back and fired again, now at a jellyfish, hooked feelers grasping at his face. The bulk of the medusa fell away and a buzz met his ears as the stinger of a large, black, striped wasp met his right eye. Screaming in rage, he swatted his hand to his face, crushing what was left of the broken soul against his face. His eyeball began to swell and soon burst, milky viscous fluid running down his face and between his fingers. From his good eye he saw a small, luminescent blue particle of light rising up into the air, small white sparks shooting from it occasionally as it rose to the heavens and disappeared.

Jules strode over to where his rifle rested, still point down into the ground. His hand still clutched the swelling right side of his face. Pulling the rifle from the dirt, he set about gathering the rest of his gear. In newfound suffering he sighed, took a step, and blinked out of existence, leaving the hills alone with the sound of the wind and the rhythmic tick-tock of the tower clock.

***

Darhmak's office sat in a giant pillared stone building near the center of Folkhill. A large dome topped the great granite structure. The rain pouring out of the thick quilt of clouds in the sky struck the Dome of Burden making it appear to weep.

Darhmak's office itself was warm and dim, lit only by a few gas lanterns adorning the dark cherry oak wall panels and a light stone lamp that sat upon Darhmak's massive desk. Though the plush leather chair Jules sat in was quite comfortable, the pain in his now empty eye-socket persisted. He sipped a mug of Bordralli ale while he awaited his superior's arrival, cursing him as he did so.

After a time Darhmak entered. "How went your hunt, Jules?" Darhmak asked in that oh-so-irritating sing-song voice of his.

Jules turned to him, pulling his hand from his face. "How does it look like it went, you contemptible old bastard?"   Darhmak grinned.

Jules rose as if to strike the withered old man in purple robes, but instead held himself back.

"Ah," Darhmak's grin grew broader, "Glad to see you remember the last time you... questioned authority."

"You should have warned me. It was shit to simply state the soul as 'Reactionary', Darhmak, and you know it."

The ancient sender made his way past him and sat down with a groan behind his desk. "I thought you'd appreciate the challenge, Jules. After all, you're the one who's always complaining of, oh what was it you said? Oh, yes, 'shepherding souls, not sending them.' I thought I was doing you a favor."

Jules glared, his face a mask of hate. "Some favor, old man. That bastard took my eye. My eye!"

Darhmak's face drooped a moment and he took a sharp intake of breath. "But you did succeed, didn't you? The soul has been sent?"

Jules cracked a sardonic smile. "I'm still ten for ten."

Darhmak set back in his high backed chair and exhaled, visibly relieved. "Good, good..." The old man seemed distracted. Almost...worried. Now Jules was on edge.

"What's going on here, Darhmak? What's got you rattled?"Darhmak snapped back to reality, focusing on the man sitting across from him. Well. Now was as good a time as any, he supposed.

"Jules," he began. "You've been here a long time now."

"Near one-hundred and ten years now, Darhmak." Jules sat back and took a long pull from his ale, the throbbing of his phantom-eye had started in again. The indelible urge to rub it, scratch it, anything to stop the burning was beginning to drive him mad, he was sure of it.

"In all that time, how many reactionary souls have you sent?"

Jules need not think to answer the question. "Five, including this one. Why?"

Darhmak rose and walked over to one of the many bookshelves lining the rear wall of his office. He reached out with both hands. His left danced along a number of file folders while his right simply disappeared into the books and shelf itself. His left hand found what it was looking for and pulled a file from the shelf, while his right slowly emerged from the illusory books and shelf holding a large jar, filled with a murky, green liquid. He tossed the file on the desk, its momentum landing it in Jules' lap, the jar he carefully set down upon his blotter pad.

Securing the file, Jules gazed with curiosity at the strange liquid within the jar. In the light of the lamp, the shadows of small creatures shown through the swirling silt. "Five. Five reactionaries in the last one-hundred and ten years, Jules. Read the file. There have been ten in the last ten months. A new reactionary each month. This was just the first we've sent your way."

Jules opened the file and tried to read it in the low light. Frowning, he looked up at Darhmak. "Can't you just sum it up for me?"

The old man was elbow deep in the jar, wincing as if being bitten, and trying to fish out one of the strange shapes eluding his grasp. Without warning he pulled his arm out and threw his catch at Jules in one fluid movement. Shouting with surprise, Jules threw a hand up to snatch the wriggling thing from the air. Keeping his hand closed tight around it, Jules began to inspect the small, wormy length of ugly he had caught. Two small pincers, like those of a crayfish, flailed about attempting to find something, anything to grasp onto. They protruded from a fleshy stalk that itself protruded from a milky orb surrounded by a translucent film.

"What in the cosmos..." Jules asked under his breath.

"Don't be daft, Jules, it's an Ocular Visinite. Jules shot Darhmak a quizzical look. Darhmak rolled his eyes and sighed . "Just bring it near your empty socket, it will do the rest quite instinctively."

Jules scoffed. "You're out of your mind, old man. I'm not letting this slimy, squirming, parasite anywhere near my fa-" Before Jules could finish, the old man was across the room and forcing Jules' own hand to his face, the Ocular Visinite thrashing wildly about.

Damn, Jules thought, *I always forget how strong this old bastard is*. Jules managed to struggle, but just for an instant, before the graybeard had brought Jules' hand and the creature to his empty ocular socket. Jules began to scream as the visinite's claws found his skin and soon the hole. He soon felt a grinding pinch somewhere in his skull as the visinite took hold inside of him.

Jules began clawing at his face. Darhmak grabbed him by the wrists. "Let me go, you crazy son of a bitch! This thing is inside me!!!" The old man held on for perhaps three breaths before finally letting go of the panicking sender. Jules' hands shot toward his face again before he froze entirely. The pain was gone. He slowly opened his right eye. Blinking, he gasped in disbelief.

Darhmak chuckled. "Amazing little oddities, aren't they?"

Jules gaped. "I...uh. I can see again. It's as if nothing ever happened to it. How?"

"Best not to ask right now. Let it grow on you first. Adjust to it. Rest assured, you'll be able to see quite well through the little monster. In fact, you may even see a bit better than before. Truth be told, this little mishap with the reactionary soul was advantageous, after a fashion. Open the file. Take a look."

Jules, still blinking against the dim light through his new... eye (?) turned the pages of the file.

Darhmak continued. "As I was saying, there has been a rash of recent reactionaries. We have no idea why or how they're growing in such numbers. We know only that they continue to be a threat to both living and separated souls." Glancing up from the pages, Jules looked at his senior.

"They're in the Prime." Darhmak grumbled, "That's the problem. It's one thing for reactionaries to be spread out across vacant planes and 'verses, but to have them running rampant throughout the Prime... Well, I don't need to tell you what's at stake."

The Prime material plane was the hub of all known planes of existence. Its presence dictated the rules for all other planes, known or otherwise. Souls separated from their hosts could not exist in the Prime. If reactionaries were gathering in the Prime, then they were breaking the rules of the universe, there, and everywhere else. There was no true way of knowing what could come of this disobedience to reality, but the theory was the complete and utter breakdown and collapse of everything. Everything that is, was, and would ever be. At least that's what the scholars predicted. Jules had never placed much faith in scholars.

Jules rose from the chair and finished his ale in a long gulp. Wiping his face with the cuff of his overcoat, he grinned at Darhmak. "I'm going to need a hell of a lot more Quicksilver."

The old man shook his head. "No need. As I was saying, losing that eye of yours was actually quite advantageous. The visinite now inhabiting your skull should have no problem discerning the trail of the reactionary souls. I understand that the trails glow with a certain hue of blue, unseen by normal eyes. We're still attempting to find out why exactly that is, how the two might be connected. But for now, we're at a loss."

Now it was Jules' turn to grumble. "What do you know about the visinites?"

Darhmak smiled. "Not a lot, but you don't look a gift horse in the mouth. What we do know is that there are dangerous reactionaries out there, and the visinites are our only sustainable way of finding them. Do you know how expensive and time consuming it is to produce Quicksilver? When we know more about them, you'll know more about them."

Jules looked down at the file in his hands. "So, which one is my new assignment?"

"All of them," Darhmak answered. "Reactionaries are your new assignment. Hunt them down. Send them. Try to keep a low profile. We'll be in touch when we need to be. Return here when you have a report to file. Or, if you're in need of more ammo." The old man's tone was dismissive and he turned to move back behind his enormous desk.

Jules grunted and turned to leave, file in hand. As he stepped out into the light of the hallway, Darhmak spoke behind him. "Jules?"

"Yeah?"

"Best of luck. And good hunting."

Jules pulled the door shut behind him.

Moon Beams and Memories Renewed
By Matthew Grubbs

"Moon Beams and Memories Revisited" comes to us from Matthew Grubbs, an amateur writer who got his start crafting science-fiction in a science-fiction and fantasy writing club. His submission for The Project is from his recent exploration into modern fantasy writing. He has many more tales in the works and hopes to publish them for your enjoyment.

Feeling a little down, Beth walked along Lake Boulevard. Everything was still at this time of night. The frantic rush from class to work and from the library to the lower union was sometimes maddening. But after the parties fizzled out and the campus went to bed (in a manner of speaking) she could finally clear her head. Sure, it might be a little dangerous, a young girl walking the streets alone at night. But it gave her time to think about things. Time to think about what she should do now. But an overcast moon gives no comfort after a break up like that. It was bad, but Brian understood. Well, he agreed. So why did she feel so damn depressed? Lifting her hands up, she gave her cheeks a slight slap. "Get a hold of yourself Bethany. There's no reason to feel like this." That's all it took for her, until she reached 10th street.

It was there the past came to meet her. A stone staircase came up from the forested shore below. The steps took you all the way down to the lake front and it was there she and Brian had their first kiss. It wasn't as romantic as it sounded. It was hot and sticky that day and the mosquitoes were out in force, buzzing and biting. Then they walked along the dirt path, trying to avoid the poison ivy and deer ticks, just to see the sun set through the tree line. It was actually the worst idea he ever had but, it seemed planned and for Brian that was saying something.

It felt like only yesterday, but really it had been a month ago today. For a month all the world seemed right and good. But those rose tinted glasses hide many things… falling grades for one. Sneaking off into the night, or day, was just impractical now that they had come so far. That she had come so far away from what she knew and from what she knew she could be. No, this was definitely better for the both of them. So why didn't it feel right? Beth walked on now, heading to where the sidewalk would lead. She slowly shuffled as she went, with the heels of her pink flares dragging on the concrete.

Beth jumped out of the way as a pair of bright blue head lamps rounded the bend and screamed off past her. She couldn't make out the plates from the ground she was now clinging to as the haze of red against the black night rumbled away. Short, staggered breaths came in and out as adrenalin pumped through her veins. Beth couldn't find the words in her mind. She couldn't find anything. Thought and instinct battled for supremacy. It was in situations like this, when you face your own mortality, that everything is supposed to become clear. All of your worries and doubts are supposed to melt away and everything that didn't make sense suddenly does. That didn't happen.

Then crystallization took her mind. The kind that happened after your life flashes before your eyes, which didn't happen. It probably didn't happen, because her life was so uneventful and she really didn't want to remember. Her 'eureka' moment was brief and left no lasting clarity or answers. So she pulled herself up, a little shakily, and kept to the path and let her thoughts fall where they may. These things rarely happen the way they do in stories. It was along the path as her thoughts rambled on, that she noticed the bench.

Made of the same concrete slab and brick, poorly mortared to form the wall on which it leaned. It was on that bench that they sat many times, her and Brian. They would talk about what they planned to do with their lives, going over Chem. notes or even reenacting Dr. Gurney's wild stories. There, on the bench that they would no longer linger upon, sat a man smoking under the glow of the street light.

His presence struck her as something of an oddity. Dressed in an unseasonably, long coat and tight black beanie. He looked so out of place, but somehow familiar. Beth couldn't quite remember who he looked like or how she might know him, so she thrust the whole situation from her mind. She had quite enough in there already and this added anomaly was not needed. She should just walk on by. There was no reason to stop. No reason to even flash a smile or a slight wave. He was a complete stranger sitting on a bench in the middle of the night. No part of that sounded safe. Every part of her intended to walk on by, but she stopped when she saw his face.

Deep brown eyes looked out beneath a long beard and an unkempt tangle of hair. Barely a mouth was visible, but a smile flashed when she drew parallel to him. As quickly as it shown, it was gone however, as if the man forgot he was supposed to be frowning. It was amazing how much he reminded her of Brain. This man could have been an uncle or a brother, raised by wolves. It was a coincidence. Brian was just on her mind and now she was projecting her issues on random strangers. He was probably just a homeless man taking a break from his walk. She knew there were a few of them migrating through the city this time of year. But surly not all of them could look like her ex.

Curiosity controlled her now as reason and logic failed her. She needed to know, but she didn't know how to say it, as the words, "Who are you?" fell from her lips.

What a terrible thing to say. Why not hello or good morning or nice night for a think? But the man only chuckled, taking a drag off his cigarette and let it out slowly. She waited for a response. Would it come? She didn't mean to say it, or rather, didn't mean to say it so bluntly, but now that it was out there he just ignored it. He just sat there... smoking. The ember burning lower with each pull he took. Each puff that he could have been saying something. After half of minute of leering, she finally gave up and turned to leave. A soft laugh followed.

"It's a very rare thing," he said letting the smoke roll out of his nose, "for me to be questioned by pretty, young girls that just happen to be walking by."

"Well, I am. Just walking by that is." Beth began then softened. That was no way to behave and she turned back to him. "I mean thank you for the compliment." That was lame. What was she doing, flirting? She didn't know this man. She didn't know what kind of person he was. Sure, he seemed kind enough, but appearances can be deceiving. Nothing seemed deceiving about him, though. Strange certainly. Unwashed, most defiantly. But for the most part he seemed harmless.

Stepping forward she held out her hand. "I'm Beth." But the man only looked up from the bench and smiled at her.

"I know."

It was such a bright smile. It wasn't attractive, with the yellow tobacco stains showing. It was genuine though and almost charming, what did he say? "That wasn't a proper response," she thought that she thought, when really she said it. Her hand moved to her lips, but it was too late. "I'm sorry," she blurted, "my day's not going too well, and I was thinking and some idiot nearly ran me over whipping around a corner."

"I know," another drag and he rolled the smoke in between his forefinger and thumb, letting the burnt ash fall to the ground before sticking the butt in his breast pocket.

"What?" She began, "How do you know about the car?"

"Because it sped by here a couple of minutes before you arrived. You look a little shaken. It doesn't take a detective to figure it out."

"Oh," she said and sighed. Everything wasn't about her and she knew that. It was just a coincidence and here she was making herself look like a babbling bimbo. She was glad she came out to clear her head and get some perspective on this whole situation. Yet, the more the night progressed the less sense it made. It certainly happens from time to time; after traumatic events, when stress has the better of your senses, when you go out for walks at 1:15 in the morning. Breathing deeply, Beth looked out over the wall and on to the lake beyond.

The wind whispered through the painted leaves of the tree line. What was once impressive, was now just trappings around a path the city kept up. A shallow homage to the past, but one that was very dear. She must have walked that path a thousand times. Looking at it now, however, it felt different. How many secret meetings did she have down in that hidden glade? How long did they look out over the rippling waters and talk? Just talk. Open and honest conversation. It was so freeing, she had to pull herself back and put those thoughts aside. She had to bury them.

A flick of flint brought Beth back from her mind as the Zippo closed behind her. Glancing behind her, she spied the man who now looked older, as if he grew with the moon and the passing of every cloud was the passing of another day. "So," she began politely, "what brings you out tonight?"

"Hm," the man nodded in a familiar way. It must have been her overactive imagination again. He took a long drag and let the smoke out slowly, enveloping his grin. "I suppose I'm here for the same reason as you."

Beth stepped back a little. Her vision and concern found the same subject in focus. "Oh, you're out here to get run over too?" she ventured. After all, a little levity never hurt anyone. It helped her out of many tense situations, the stressful conversations and especially Christmas with her mother's side of the family. Though as experience taught, she wasn't very good at it. Maybe he wouldn't take it seriously.

"No, I'm just here for a think and, like you, home really isn't an option."

She let that comment go by. Dwelling upon it was none of her business and she didn't want to be rude. He had his reasons for being here just like she did. Maybe he had something just as deep pulling at him. Maybe his mistakes kept his feet to the ground, walking the path between regret and denial. She had to admit that she could be stubborn when she wanted to be. Being tenacious was no shortcoming. But it did make things harder than they had to be. She didn't know his reasons and that was the way she wanted to keep it. She was searching for something to say now. Something that wouldn't offend, yet kept in line with the conversation. "Why do you put them in your pocket?"

"What?" The man looked up in surprise after he tucked the second butt away. "Oh, habit, I guess."

He didn't like to litter. Killing his body he could handle, but not defacing the planet. He was conscientious, certainly, but impassive. It must have been his nature and new questions filled her head. There were so many similarities it couldn't be coincidence.

"Alright," he said, standing up and stretching. "It's time for me to get back."

"Get back? Wait, but, now?"

"Yeah, it's been a long time since I was out and got to think. It was nice to be back here, but I must be going. It was nice to see you."

"Yes, and you too," she said, standing back to give him space to depart. A smile touched her eyes and her hand half raised in a wave. Didn't he mean meet? It was nice to meet me? "Wait," she called after he had taken a few paces. "What's your name?"

"Me," he said, lighting another smoke and lifting his head to the sky. "I'm just a figment of your imagination." Walking away, he raised a hand in the air. "Take care of yourself, Bethany Rae. I hope you have a safe walk back."

She waited, rooted to the spot; the questions came to rest along with a very important observation. "Wait," she raced after him nearly falling as her pants got caught on the bench. "Wait," she called, but he was already approaching Rotary Park. She ran past the water treatment grate only to reach the trees along the beach. "How did you know...?" But he was gone, melted into the fog as if he never had been there to begin with.

Disillusioned, she walked back. Her mind and feet working at a snails' pace, she tried to piece together the events that had just happened. The real and the surreal played as twin dance partners, brothers, fighting over the attention of the same girl, her. Her mind felt heavier than it had before last week's midterm and events and facts were less clear. It wasn't until she found herself back at the bench did she attempt to rationalize.

But no, even the ashes had blown away after a quick examination. A hole had formed in her line of thinking that she couldn't fill. Nothing could be the same now and she realized that's the way it should be. The clouds passed away and Luna's face shown in her full glory. New prospects about possibility reached her as a lingering smile spread from ear to ear. She had her moment of clarity. Not bothering to glance at her watch she reached into her pocket and pulled out her phone. "No time like the present." She said laughing at her own joke and dialed the familiar number she couldn't bring herself to erase.

34

The Reset Button
By Benjamin Wilcox

Benjamin Wilcox is an attorney in a small town in West Central Minnesota, where he lives with his wife and children. He has been writing novels and short stories as a hobby for the past 18 years. Other hobbies include reading, gaming, camping, playing and writing music, and spending time with his family. With all this on his plate, we are pleased he found the time to write, "The Reset Button" for our premier issue.

Beginnings are made up of two parts fear, one part wonder, and three parts confusion. Sometimes the ratios differ, but that usually seems to be the way it works. From that first new job to those first days in a blossoming relationship, there's a little "oh, crap", even less "oh wow", and a whole lot of "what the hell?"

This is a story about how I met my beautiful soul mate. I guess you could call it something of a love story. Like every story, I suppose I should start at the beginning.

My name is Adam Jensen. Before the week I met my beloved Evangeline, I had no idea what I was doing with myself. I wasn't a bad person. I lived alone in a studio apartment in a close suburb of Minneapolis. I worked as a bank teller, which was unfortunately the best thing I could do with a music degree and not much in the way of other, more practical skills. By night, I played drums for a not-even-close-to-successful-but-completely-awesome local band, whenever we could get a gig. Usually that meant Tuesday night, starting at Midnight, at one of the many local bars that were gracious enough to host "local band night". On nights that I wasn't playing, I was usually out about town, checking out a friend's band and supporting the local music scene.

That was the situation on the night in question; the night that completely changed my life. My friend Jason was playing guitar in his band, Human Buttbox (and I swear to God band names will continue to get worse and worse as the world gets more and more of them) and I was one of maybe five or six people in the audience. The music was generic but tight, and Rolling Rock was on special. I'd only had a couple of beers, and I knew I had to get out of there before I became a wreck in the morning. It was Thursday night, and work always came way too early.

I stepped out into a bright Minnesota winter night. My breath frosted from my mouth, and I looked up at the Minneapolis sky, all blue and purple from the reflected city lights. Every sound seems louder on a winter night, and everything seems like it's packed in close and warm, holding its breath and waiting for spring. My footsteps echoed across the pavement as I walked to my car. I fumbled in the pocket of my jeans until I was able to withdraw the key with my clumsy freezing fingers, and I hit the unlock button and started the chore of scraping the frost off of my windows while my car warmed up.

I got in and started heading for home. When I was about two blocks from the club, I saw the most beautiful girl I'd seen in years, standing on the curb. She was wearing a light jacket and no hat, and her long blonde hair whipped behind her on the windy night. She was waving at my car as I pulled up to the stop sign next to her. I glanced in my rear-view mirror to see if there was someone behind me that she was waving to. There were no other cars back there. A few others zipped by on the busier cross-street in front of me, but nothing behind me. This girl was frantically waving to me, and the look on her face said that she wasn't having a good night.

Her face was totally disarming, her rosy cheeks and pale skin, cold and beautiful. I rolled my passenger side window down.

"Hey dude, you've gotta help me out," she said. She had the hint of an accent, like something Eastern European or maybe South African, barely enough to notice but definitely there. "My car won't start. Do you have any jumper cables?"

I had a set in my car. Something about the situation was making the hair on the back of my neck stand up, but I pushed it down and tried not to make it obvious that I was completely checking this girl out. "Uh…yeah," was all I was able to say. "Where's your car?"

"It's a couple of blocks from here," she replied.

"Hop in," I said. "I'll take you there if you just tell me where to go." She got in the car and pointed directions to me.

"What's your name?" I asked with a tremor in my voice that was more than just the cold.

"Natalie," she replied. It was a nice enough name, if you could get past the Facts of Life reference.

We drove for a couple of blocks into a much darker part of town. I didn't see any cars on the street, except one that had no wheels and broken windows, and looked as if it had been sitting there since the late 70s. "Where's your car?" I asked.

"It's just in there," she said, and pointed to a dark alley. That feeling at the back of my neck turned into a coldness deeper than the winter air. Of course it was a dark alley. Everything in me started screaming that this was not going to end well. But Natalie was just so…damned cute.

Obviously my concern was plain on my face. "Look, I really appreciate this," Natalie said, and rested her hand on my leg. Sometimes it's really sickening how simply a woman can break a man's will. I drove into the alley.

There was a car there, parked in the corner. It was a newer car, a very *Natalie*-seeming car, and my inhibitions went out the window. She was really parked here, and I was helping a damsel in distress. I would be rewarded. There would be karma. There would be good feelings. There would be a beautiful woman wrapping her naked self around me in pure gratitude. All would be well. She got out of the car.

She started walking toward her car and it was all I could do not to stare as she walked ahead of me. Scratch that, I was unabashedly staring. She was lit by my headlights and swayed toward her car with the grace of a viper, and her jeans were *very* tight. My heart felt like it was going to burst out of my chest and start trying to kill Sigourney Weaver.

I pulled the hood of my car up to hers and stepped out into the night air. I popped the trunk and moved around to dig for my jumper cables. As I bent my head into the trunk, I became aware that there were at least four other people surrounding me. I jumped up and tried to turn around, but I wasn't fast enough. The last thought I had before I got clocked in the head by something hard and wooden was that I was a complete and total chump, and should remember not to trust beautiful women.

Nighty night.

Waking up from that unconsciousness wasn't what I would have expected. Sure, I had a massive headache that throbbed harder than the worst plastic bottle hangover I'd ever experienced. I was foggy and dizzy and not fully aware of my surroundings, so I guess that matched what I would have expected as well. Slowly, though, the world around me began to take shape, my thoughts started following one another like ants in a file, and I started getting more and more confused about where I was.

The first memories to return were following Natalie to her car and getting jumped. Obviously some muggers had knocked me in the head. My next curious thought was confusion, because I was obviously indoors and warm. The third thought was that I could still feel my wallet in my pants in the chair that I was sitting in. The fourth thought was that said chair seemed an awful lot like some sort of dentist's chair. Fifth, I thought it was strange that I was in a chair at all, and not on the cold ground somewhere. Sixth, I realized to my horror that my hands and feet were strapped to the chair, and that no amount of pulling or struggling was going to break the straps. Finally, as my eyes cleared enough to notice that the light in the room was really bright; I noticed that there were four men in the room with me, all of whom were wearing lab coats.

"What the hell?" I tried to whisper, but all that really came out was, "Whargle ghe?"

"Try to relax, Mr. Jensen," said one of the lab coat men. I couldn't quite make out his face because of the intense light behind him, but his voice reminded me of a stuffy college professor. "There's no point trying to break the straps, so you might as well stop being so tense. We'll explain everything." His voice was maddeningly calm.

Another of the lab coat brigade stepped forward. When he spoke, his voice betrayed a thin veneer of merry old England. "Mr. Jensen, I'm going to get right to the point. The world is a mess, and we're going to go ahead and end it." Yep, Merry Old England Man didn't beat around the bush, but that did nothing to end my confusion.

"Yes," said Mr. Calm, "we're going to push the reset button," he said, as if gamer terminology was going to make it any easier for me to understand.

"Who are you?" I managed to ask.

"That's fairly unimportant," said Mr. Brit, "but I'll tell you anyway. We're part of the United States Government. We're an organization that prefers, for reasons that will become obvious to you, to remain under the radar.

"You see, the United States has become a bit too big for its britches. If you've studied any history, you know that empires that get too large inevitably collapse. Prime examples include the Roman Empire, the Persians, the Babylonians, and the British Empire. The United States doesn't want this to happen, but understands that if things continue as they are, a collapse will happen.

"What we've decided to do, therefore, is to simply end all other government."

My confusion had only grown, and I started thinking about how I was going to make my escape. There was just no conceivable reason that this crazy story could possibly relate to me.

"Don't worry," said Mr. Calm, "It'll all make sense. First we need to inoculate you. I'm afraid this is going to hurt quite a bit."

It did. I felt a needle that had to be the size of a chisel jab into the back of my neck. The sensation that followed was something like being set on fire from the inside, followed by being trampled by a football team. I'm not going to lie, I screamed. I don't know how long the pain lasted, but eventually I realized that I had stopped screaming and was just sort of sitting in the chair, blubbering.

"Here's what we're going to do, Mr. Jensen," said Mr. Calm. His voice had started to ooze a bit, and although I couldn't make him out in front of the bright light, I started to imagine that this was what a talking snake might sound like. "We're going to kill everybody on Earth. I don't say this for shock value or because I'm evil. I say this because it's the only solution to our problem."

The weight of his words crept over me like a shroud. I was inoculated. For some reason I couldn't comprehend, I was going to live through this. But my family, my friends, everyone else I knew…

I realized that tears had started leaking from my eyes as the magnitude of the evil standing before me manifested itself.

"We've inoculated approximately 200 people on Earth against the virus that will be released in eight hours," said Mr. Calm. "These people, yourself included, will be dropped in chosen areas on Earth. We expect that some others will survive the virus, but the population of the Earth will be all but eradicated. We'll leave it to you few survivors to start over.

"The rest of us are leaving Earth. Where we're going won't make any difference to you, because you won't be able to get there. Understand, however, that we'll be observing you as you live out your life. I'm not going to lie to you; the people leaving will be important government officials from around the world, and other influential people. You won't see us again.

"You and the other survivors were chosen because your hospital records have indicated that you'll have the best chance of survival and procreation. You will be taken to remote locations around the globe and left there to fend for yourselves. I suspect that eventually you'll seek out the old hubs of civilization, but that by the time you reach them, there will be little of use to you.

Locations have been chosen close to the equator based on factors such as ease of survival and difficulty of finding your way back to anywhere worth mentioning.

"Mr. Jensen, we wish you the best of luck. Goodbye."

The light in the room slowly faded, and my last thought was that I'd been drugged.

I woke slowly to the sound of lapping waves and the light of bright sunshine. I blinked my eyes and stood up. I was on a beach somewhere, and it was beautiful.

Memories of my evening came pounding back into my head, and tears started to flow. There was nothing I could do. I was stuck on some deserted island, and for all intents and purposes was literally the last person I'd ever see on Earth. I spent two hours praying that this was some cruel joke or reality TV show.

Above the lapping waves, I heard the sound of someone sobbing. It sounded like a girl. I got up and walked around a curve in the beach, and saw her.

This girl looked like she'd had about as bad a night as I had. She was lithe and blond, probably in her early twenties, and sat on the beach wearing a pair of jeans and a t-shirt and sobbing into her hands. She didn't stop crying as I walked up.

"Hello?" I said carefully. Her head whipped up and a look of confusion replaced the look of sorrow.

"Um, hi?" she said.

"I guess they didn't leave us to die alone," I said.

That look of sorrow made its way back onto her face, and I felt like crying myself.

"Mind if I sit here?" I asked.

"Knock yourself out," she replied.

I plopped into the sand next to her and looked out over the crystal blue of the ocean, idly wondering where we were. It looked like it might be somewhere in the Caribbean, but it could be a Greek island for all I knew.

A sound started building above the waves as we sat silently looking at the ocean, and that sound eventually developed into a roar. Lines of light appeared in the sky, and I realized that I was looking at the trails of hundreds of rockets, blasting into space.

"Whoa," I said.

"Yeah," said the girl next to me, "Looks like they weren't kidding." The weight of that statement was immense. Her voice didn't waver, and it looked like her crying had ended, for the time being at least.

"I'm Adam, by the way," I said hesitantly.

She burst into laughter. It wasn't just a giggle, it was a hearty belly-laugh that sounded like it was just shy of all-out insanity.

"What's so funny?" I asked during a pause in her laughter.

She looked at me and wiped a tear from her eye. "Nice to meet you, Adam," she said, still struggling to contain her laughter, "My name's Evangeline. My friends call me Eve.

Frosty the Old Man
By Shannon Monkley

"Frosty the Old Man" by Shannon Monkley, is a lovely piece of creative non-fiction. A mechanic by day, he writes and paints in his free time. He began writing in high school and now continues to write as a hobby. He hopes to continue submitting for publication and someday write a novel.

It smelled of rain as I unlocked the door leading to my pride and joy. Being an entrepreneur meant horrible morning hours with few breaks, followed by a grueling afternoon without any at all. Discarding the rain and the misgivings of owning my own business with the morning mail, bills mostly, I made my way to the back of the store. It was a Wednesday, and as such no one would be in to bother me. Which was just as well, as I had ledgers to update and taxes to file. This day would be eye numbing.

It was no surprise to me when the clock tolled 10, telling me that my day was over. I had covered over half the year's receipts this day, and was on pace to allow myself a weekend off. The surprise came when I opened the front door and stepped into two inches of fresh snow. The rain I had foreseen earlier had turned in the late October weather.

Being a native, and by choice no less, lends me the heart to deal with the first snow as it should be dealt with. I scooped up a nice handful, packed it quite neatly, and waited for a car to pass. At my

age, no one would suspect the missile. It would be the perfect crime. After a
few seconds I realized my folly: No cars would be on the road at this time of night. Not on a Wednesday, anyway. Thursday maybe, as Bill had his 'all you can eat' shrimp fry at the Legion on Thursdays. I let my palm get halfway open before the idea struck. It had been years since I had built a snowman. Tonight I would. And it would be a great one.

      The snow leant itself to the work. It takes a very special type of snow to create a good snowman, as any snowman veteran will tell you. It cannot be too dry or too wet, and must possess in it a type of sticky coarseness, like frozen Elmer's glue.

      The base is the most important part. It must be wide enough to support the trunk and perfectly round save for the top and bottom. If the snowman is to have any respect, the base must be at least three feet in diameter. Mine would be four.

      Giggles rang in my left ear as I bent down to roll the base. I looked across the street to see three young children. All of them were boys. At least, I estimated them as such, snowsuits being the great androgynous garb. The two larger boys, under the direction of the third, were building their own snowman, directly across the road from mine. The larger ones strained to gather as much of the snow as they could before it melted into two large piles. I assumed they would then form these piles into the first two sections of their man, adding the head after the two others had been sculpted. It was not a bad plan, but would take far longer to do, and with less efficient results than mine. The smaller boy must have expressed sentiment much the same, as he pointed in my direction and mimicked my actions with his hands. The two Neanderthals, unaccustomed as they must be to taking orders, cast out the third and continued with their original plan.

That was all the motivation I needed. Being the smaller, and more intelligent, boy in my own time made me sympathize with this young man's plight. How often he, as I once was, must have been picked last for recess games and be picked on by the likes of the two big bullies. I would teach them a lesson. I would build my snowman first, and I would build it larger. They would have to see their plan as inferior if an old fart like me outdid them.

I mustered every ounce of creativity I had as I rolled the ever-growing trunk of my man around the snow. Tracks of dirty grass lay in my wake until finally I had my base. Without pause I moved on to the torso, taking snow from every inch of land I could find.

A quick glance over my shoulder told me the bullies were on my heels. I redoubled my efforts and soon was rewarded with a large, semi brown torso. The head was not an issue, as I had planned ahead enough to leave myself a prime patch of snow just around the building. Once in place, I stared at my new creation. It looked exactly like what it was: three balls of snow atop each other. It was almost perfect in its design, yet lacked the essence of a snowman. It had no coal eyes, no carrot nose, nor a corncob pipe.

Having none of these items on hand, I ran as quickly as I could to the convenience store. Two cookies from the day-old bakery shelf would serve as eyes. The nose would be a 20 oz bottle of diet Pepsi (I planned on drinking it first). Of course, every C-Store worth its weight stocks pipes, so that was not an issue.

At the counter was a stand of sunglasses. They were the cheap stock variety found at every counter top in America, and no respectable person would be caught dead buying them. But my snowman had no such qualms. He would look very cool with the shades over his eyes. The cookies would be moved down his body and serve as buttons for his imaginary coat.

I ran as fast as I could back to my corner. The boys across the street were rolling around what looked to be the head, and I knew I had plenty of time. I did not see the smaller boy, and assumed the other two had run him off. My fire rekindled inside me as I put the newly purchased parts of my snowman onto his face and body. Caught up in the fervor of building, I even added my own scarf to his neck. Some pine sprigs became his arms, and my snowman was complete. He stood just shy of five feet tall, and was the most amazing snowman I had ever laid eyes upon.

A shout of glee from across the road told me the boys had finished as well. I looked at their creation: It stood around three feet, was lopsided, and wore nothing but a hat from the biggest boy's head. They had finished just as I had, and that was all that mattered to them.

I would have walked home just then, but something happened. The smaller boy was back on the scene, shovel in tow, and was walking out into the street. Both boys shared my astonishment as the small one carefully shoveled the snow from the road into neat little patches.

When about ten of them were made he started his process. Each patch of snow was harvested, five for the base, three for the torso, and two for the head. Every flake of snow was used and in no time a two-foot snowman was born. The street became a proud mother, holding its babe out for the world to see. The thing was more of a slush man, built of an odd mix of grimy road salts and snow. But it was perfect in its structure and design, and was a terribly beautiful thing to look at.

But for the want of my body to be in my bed, I would have marveled at this scene for hours. The two boys had retired to bed, but the third stood watch from the corner until my legs directed me away. I took one last look at our creations. The two white snowmen stood as sentinels over the slush-man in the middle of the road. There the holy precession would stand until morning, long after the world had gone to bed. As I walked off, the little boy draped his jacket around the body of his work. I smiled.

I awoke with aching joints and eager mind. I needed desperately to check on our sculptures from the night before. I jogged the four blocked to my store as early as I could, skipping breakfast and a shower. I needn't have worried. Less the light of the moon and street lamps casting a yellow glow, the scene remained the same. My snowman had lost a bit of mass to the night, as had the other two. But all three stood as they did when I had left the night before. I was proud.

My mind woke to the sound of a car. This was not good, as the slush man stood directly in the main thoroughfare of the business district. My snowman was safe, as was its smaller counterpart, but the outcast slush man was headed for a collision. The car neared the snowman, and the two were locked in an eternal struggle. About fifty feet before impact, however, the car slowed and carefully rounded the man, leaving it intact. Each car behind acted in kind as the trickle of city life began to flood the shops. The passer-bys would stop to point and then lower heads and continue with the business of the day.

I conveniently forgot to open my shop and took a post on a bench opposite the scene. Throughout the day I watched as car after car avoided the slowly melting slush monster in the road. On the other side of the street I saw the creator of the man from the night before.

Shivering in the cold, jacket given to the cause, the builder stood quietly. In those eyes was something great. They held a sense of accomplishment and contentment few others could boast.

Then a heard a sound that threw my heart into my stomach. It was the familiar beep and scrape of the plow, come to make the rounds.   With a slow and deliberate roll, the slush man died. No one noticed except me, and the little boy. He recovered much faster than I did. With eyes still full of glitter he walked into the middle of the road, picked his jacket from the slush, gave it two brisk shakes, and returned it to his shoulders. The thing was dirty and wet, but never had a jacket fit a child so well. He smiled at me, as if thanking me for sharing this moment, and then gave me a puzzled look. It was if he was asking me why I was still attached to the scene. What's done is done, his eyes spoke to me. I could only stare.

It was then a slush ball hit me in the ear. It came from the hands of the small child. With a gap-toothed, grin he smiled briefly and then ran away, small legs pumping as fast as snow would allow. It was the perfect crime.

The Commonwealth
by Eric Kuha

A part-time instructor at a North Dakota community college, Eric Kuha is an avid science-fiction fan who enjoys exploring the versatility of the genre in his writing. He hopes you will enjoy his latest creation, "The Commonwealth".

It is Thursday evening, just as the cicadas are waking up and starting to make their first tentative chirps at the retreating sun. Folks who've known each other their entire lives spend another perfect July evening on the porch drinking beer or iced tea while watching the kids play in the yard. But something altogether different is going on at 245 Birch Street. In the basement, a man is giving his wife an anniversary gift.

It has a red bow tied around it. In just a few months, it will change many lives. It is the sort of thing that becomes the reference point. It has a force that is great, not because of what it is, for it is not unique at all. Its potency is derived from the meaning that a small community will eventually define it with.

"What is it?" says Malcolm's wife as a large, white sheet is stripped from the object that sits on the workbench like an oversized paperweight.

"It's a nuclear warhead," says Malcolm to his wife—Shilly is her name—who stares in wonderment at the cone with the large red bow tied around it. A perfect, red rose lies in front of it on the bench.

"How ever did you get it?" she asks, approaching it and running a fingertip from the top of the cone, over the very potent, bright yellow radiation icon, to its twelve inch, circular base.

"I stole it. It's really for the family. Home protection."

"You stole it?" she says, walking around it and finally seeing the letters US followed by a serial number.

"Yeah, I mean, it's only about a hundred kilotons, but I figure that's a pretty good entry level atomic bomb."

Shilly frowns at the device.

"You know, an opportunity presented itself. It'll be great for the family, and since our anniversary was coming up, and there it was, I decided to make it an anniversary gift. Happy anniversary, sweetie."

"Malcolm," she says, sternly, looking directly at her husband. "I love it," she says, breaking into a smile and throwing her arms around his neck, kissing him repeatedly.

Malcolm and Shilly make love that evening while the children play Monopoly in the living room, a nuclear warhead sitting quietly on their father's workbench in the basement.

"You know," says Howser, sipping from his can of American beer, "the country's nuclear stockpile is aging. If I were to wager a guess, I'd say this thing is maybe twenty or thirty years old. Who's to say it even works anymore? How do you know it was only in that warehouse on its way to be dismantled?"

Burke breaks in, "Howser, what kinda shit are you talking anyway? No way this one's that old. One that small has gotta be new. Maybe five years."

Howser says, "Ah-ha! But they haven't even made any new bombs in over ten years. Ipso facto, no way it can be newer'n that."

"Well, how long does a nuclear bomb last, anyhow?" asks Burke.

"'Bout twenty years, I'd wager," says Howser.

"Then this one's probably fine! It's only ten years old."

"I said it couldn't be any less than ten. It's probably a lot older. And it was made of shitty Cold War materials. It's probably just a bunch of junk."

"Look," says Malcolm. "It's just for show anyway, guys. No way I'd use it. I don't even know how to use it, and I don't think that testing it is a good idea." He pauses, taking a sip from his can of beer. "What with only having one of them and all."

"I could get it working, Mal. Just give me a couple hours. I'll take it apart, see what wires go to the detonator, and I could set you up with a switch that'll blow it."

"You do *not* know how to make a nuclear bomb work," says Burke. "There's a reason they called Einstein an atomic scientist and you an electrician."

"I do so know how to make this thing work. It's a cinch. Just google it. It's all on the internet. I can make *you* a nuclear bomb, Burke. Not that I ever would, what with you being such an asshole."

"Guys, guys," says Malcolm. "It's alright. It's nice of you to offer, Howser, but just the same, for the time being, I'm going to just keep it as is, and I'd ask you guys to do me a favor and just keep this under your hat, okay? Just don't tell no one."

"What are you talking about?" says Howser. "You're missing the whole point of owning a nuclear weapon!"

"And what is that, Howser?" asks Burke.

"It's a deterrent! The person with the most nukes is the most powerful person. In this case, as the sole nuclear power in the whole town, you are, by default, the most powerful man in... probably the whole damned county! But it ain't no good if you keep it a secret! Nukes aren't 'secret weapons,' Mal. They're to be flaunted and lied about. In fact," he says, becoming ever more insistent, "instead of telling people that you only have one, you should tell them that you have two!"

Again, Malcolm speaks up, calm as you please, "Just the same, boys, I want this to be just between us. For now," he adds, as a conciliatory measure.

"But--" says Howser.

"For now," says Mal. "You think you can keep this quiet? Can I trust you assholes to keep your damned mouths shut about this thing?"

"Of course," says Burke.

"Sure, fine," says Howser. "We won't tell no one."

"Did you know that Malcolm has a nuclear warhead?" Howser asks his wife—Diane—that evening.

"You don't say," says Diane Howser, putting her hair up in curlers.

After that, it is only a matter of a few days before the entire town knows. Diane Howser tells Mrs. Blake who goes for her perm on Monday and tells the gals at the salon who tell their husbands who tell their fishing buddies who tell their wives who already know.

There is a small Air Force base south of town. Malcolm had recently landed an extremely lucrative contract to pour some concrete pads and gut and refurbish a warehouse. For two weeks, Malcolm was waved onto the base without a search.

It was, perhaps, a stroke of genius to put those nukes there. It's right in the middle of a field in the center of a tiny military base in the focal point of all things Midwest. Nobody would ever look for nukes there, and, more importantly, no one would attack there. Seriously, all they'd have to do is keep it locked and no one would ever bother to break in.

And so, it is maybe just a little funny that the biggest fuck-up in military history actually happened years ago when somebody *forgot* to lock the door to this warehouse.

Malcolm had found a side door unlocked when he was searching for an officer to whom he could complain about the absurd requirement that they keep all of the sod that they dug up as intact as possible and stack it up off to the side on pallets. He was *not* a landscaper, dammit, and this was *not* in his contract. Not to mention being the dumbest thing he'd ever heard. If they want the sod so damned bad, they should just buy new anyway.

He had stepped into the warehouse and shouted a few "Hellos" and squinted into the musty darkness. The warehouse was utterly deserted but for a line of pallets in the center of the room. On those pallets were heavy-looking latched crates. They were old and layered with dust.

Curiosity had overcome him and he had approached the crates and read the stenciled letters on the sides of them. He had spotted the symbol for radioactivity.

It was a couple days later when he returned with two trusted employees, a truck, and a crowbar. They walked right inside, completely unobserved by anyone who would have known what was in the warehouse, busted open one of the crates and wrestled one of the cone-shaped warheads into the back of his truck and covered it with a tarp. He had awarded each of his helpers with a thousand dollar bonus to keep their damned mouths shut. He didn't want Shilly finding out before their anniversary.

It is a few days after their anniversary and Malcolm has been thinking. The whole town knows about the nuke now and perhaps it is time to go public with it. He approaches Howser with a proposition: "I've got a six-pack for you if you come over and make it work."

He has no way of knowing that at that exact moment, a local flyboy who likes to hang around at the town bars and had caught wind of the world's first domestically owned weapon of mass destruction, is informing the Master Sergeant of the rumor.

As Howser arrives in Malcolm's basement with a cardboard box full of supplies and a toolbox, the Master Sergeant is passing the rumor on to his

Captain, who immediately calls the Lieutenant Colonel who, he never fails to remind the Master Sergeant, is a personal friend.

Malcolm and Howser are taking apart the device at about the time that the Lieutenant Colonel is assuming that he has just been told a hysterical new joke. "This is not a joke," says the Captain, feeling nervous.

"'Course it's a joke. That's the goddamned craziest thing I've ever heard and I've been in the *Air Force* for thirty-five years."

"This rumor is very pervasive. Everyone here seems to believe it."

"Okay smartass, then why haven't I seen anything about a nuclear scare? Where's the news?"

"The thing is, sir, nobody seems to be all that concerned about it."

"What?!"

"The locals seem to support him."

Howser sets Malcolm up with a detonator. It is a remote, he says, that will detonate the nuke from anywhere within five miles of Malcolm's home. Malcolm nods sagely after they break into the promised six-pack. Malcolm heads up to his computer to draft a press release for the paper.

The next day, the Joint Chiefs are meeting with The President who says, "What?!"

"He is seceding from the union, sir. Just up to his property line, he says. He wants international recognition and to open trade negotiations."

"He contacted us?"

"No, he just sent a press release to his local paper."

"And he claims to be a nuclear power?"

"That's what the press release says."

"Have any nukes gone missing?"

"We've got people doing an inventory. Nothing's turned up missing yet."

"Send some agents. Snoop around that town and find out just what the hell's going on there. I've got bigger things to deal with."

"Yes, Mr. President."

Howser and Burke live right next door to Malcolm on either side. Malcolm and Shilly invite them and their wives over for dinner a day after the remote detonator was constructed out of some parts from a cellphone and an old amateur radio kit. Turns out, Howser is also a HAM radio nut. Of all things.

Shilly says to Mrs. Howser—Diane—that she is very impressed with the begonias this year.

"Oh, thank you Shilly. I've been using coffee grounds mixed with egg shells. It's wonderful!"

"Does that work?" asks Shilly, genuinely fascinated.

"The proof is in my garden!" says Diane.

Mrs. Burke—Evie—says, "Listen to this! Trading garden tips with a foreign dignitary."

Shilly waves a hand and says, "Oh stop. Just because we live in another country doesn't mean we aren't still neighbors, Evie. And while we're on the subject, Malcolm and I have something we want to ask you."

"What's this, Mal?" says Howser around a mouthful of Shilly's fantastic pot roast.

"You sure, Shilly?" asks Mal.

"You can tell them, honey. It's a great idea."

"Well," says Mal, leaning back in his chair, "we were kinda thinking that running a country is a lot of work. Thought maybe we could use a hand. Been thinking of maybe annexing your houses and yards into Malcolmia."

"Is that the name you settled on, dear?" asks Shilly.

"Something I've been toying with. You like it?"

"A little egocentric, don't you think?"

"So it is, Darling. So it is."

"So wait," says Burke, "You trying to conquer us, or what?"

"Well," says Malcolm, "we were hoping for a peaceful annexation. Titles and estates will be granted, of course."

"What do you mean?" asks Burke.

"Well, since I'm Lord Regent of the country and Shilly here is Lady Regent, I figured you'd both be lords of your own houses. Your manors, I mean, if you want to get technical. Since it would be annexed to our country, you will be granted full custody of your land and houses. Of course, once annexed, it would be my land, which I would then award to you in return for your loyal service to the country." Malcolm laughs suddenly, "When I told the bank I wasn't going to pay my mortgage anymore, you should have heard the huffing and the puffing. We still owe about a thirty or so on the house. What are they going to do, though? We've got the nuke."

Mrs. Burke says, "Well, I think we'll have to give it some thought. I mean. How far out are you planning on expanding?"

"Just you guys for now. We might just conquer the Hopwells across the street. They're a bunch of jackasses and their Tod's been bullying Adrienne for weeks. If they're part of our country then maybe we can put 'em in their place. Not gonna evict 'em or anything. Just rein them in. They've been terrorizing and monopolizing the neighborhood committee for far too long. Easement statutes my ass."

"Well, we'll think it over tonight," says Mrs. Howser. "Tomorrow's Sunday, so we'll let you know at church."

"Deal," says Malcolm. "What's for dessert, honey?"

"Strawberry rhubarb pie!" says Shilly.

A murmur of anticipation ripples around the table. A sense of excitement is in the air, and the pie is only half of it.

Agents Lister and Townsend roll into town at about 11:30 AM Sunday, just as church is getting out for all the folks that go to the contemporary service. They stop at a local diner and both order the Denver omelet and copies of the local fishwrapper. The Sunday paper has a feature piece on the Lord Regent of the new nation which, thus far, has no official name. It is, in large part, biographical, highlighting Malcolm's days as quarterback of the high school team and their ultimately unsuccessful bid for the state title his senior year. It goes on from there to mention how he married his high school sweetheart, Shilly, and how they and their son and two daughters have been model citizens of the town, Malcolm running M&M Construction with his partner and neighbor Marty Howser, and how Shilly works part-time as a nurse at the old folks' home.

The story moves on from there to talk about some of Malcolm's peaceful gestures toward the community as Lord Regent. Habitat for Humanity has signed a contract for two houses to be built. Malcolm makes it a point to emphasize his "foreign policy" particularly as pertains to "foreign aid" in "underdeveloped nations."

Malcolm says that their kids will still attend the local elementary school in the fall, but for now, they are adjusting to life as prince and princesses. Malcolm "jokes," the paper says, that it won't be the first time that nobility will send their children to school abroad to get the best education possible.

There is some dissent, the story goes on, amongst some members of the community, mostly on the part of the bank, on the grounds that Malcolm has claimed he intends to default on his mortgage, claiming that the property is now foreign soil and, as part of getting a new nation up and running, funds need to be spent elsewhere. The existing foreign debt, Malcolm claims, ought to be outright forgiven, especially on account of the fact that Malcolm did the bank president's driveway for half the price of any other bids.

There is mention of a number of royal decrees, mostly involving property egress rules in his neighborhood covenant and the location of Malcolm's tool shed.

Agents Lister and Townsend finish reading the story at almost the exact same time as their meals arrive. They eat, drink coffee, discuss various theories—mostly about the validity of claims that Malcolm has an atomic bomb—and head out, leaving the waitress a very nice tip, which she spends on a new haircut.

In the fellowship hall, after the service, members of the congregation of First Lutheran are drinking coffee. Many topics are discussed, but perhaps the most common topic is Pastor Gastor's sermon. Lord Regent Malcolm was the subject of the homily, and, while this was to be expected— Pastor Gastor is widely known to have his finger on the pulse of the community or, depending on your opinion of him, to be a notorious gossip hound—the fact that Pastor Gastor gave Malcolm a personal *blessing* was a little shocking. Malcolm is doing the Lord's work, he had said, starting fresh, defining a new kingdom where the people walk in the light of Christ's love. Or some such. The actual words change much as the people repeat "the gist" of what Pastor Gastor had said.

In the end, the conclusion that folks come to is that if Malcolm has the blessings of Pastor Gastor, then he must be doing right by the community. A few folks even start to discuss the possibility of petitioning for annexation.

The days go by. By mid-July, half of the town is part of the new nation, generally known as the Commonwealth. Its borders incorporate the super market *and* First Lutheran Church. Pastor Gastor has petitioned the ELCA for a new regional synod to be founded in the Commonwealth and modestly suggested himself to be its bishop. The petition is scheduled to be considered by the Church wide Assembly this fall.

Agents Lister and Townsend have become known by face and name to the populace and the lords and ladies of the Commonwealth are, to the agents' surprise, very open and friendly and utterly honest with the agents. After all, they say, we are a nuclear power. What are you going to do to stop us?

They are granted an audience with the Lord Regent, but not access to the Bomb Room—Malcolm's basement and central headquarters. For all they are able to tell, the guy is completely sane, just...not.

There are a couple of messy incidents. In the interests of keeping the Commonwealth's borders contiguous, a few houses have to be annexed forcefully. Conquered, is the word commonly used by the townsfolk. Nobody is seriously injured beyond pride and, if a few bumps and scrapes during an invasion are all, then most folks are fine with it. You gotta nurture a new country as it grows.

After a while, whole blocks are getting annexed in one shot. As downtown gets eaten up over the course of three days, business owners start hanging signs outside saying, "Hail Lord Regent Malcolm!" In a fit of one-ups-manship, Harv, the hardware store owner hangs a sign that says "*All* Hail Lord Regent Malcolm."

Old Smiley's Saloon is renamed "Malcolm's Place" in honor of the Lord Regent, and even manages to see an appreciable increase in beer sales as a result.

It's July 17th, when the borders of the Commonwealth go right up to the main branch of the First National Bank, which saw the first of many defaulted loans just a few weeks ago. Oh sure, they aren't technically in default yet, but so many titles and estates have been granted by the Lord Regent, that the bank is worried that it might never see another dime.

As a conciliatory gesture, Lord Regent Malcolm sets up a meeting with the Board of Directors of First National Bank. The mood in the board room is tense and expectant. Lord Regent Malcolm, dressed in all the splendor of his station, takes a seat at the far end of the table, opposite the bank President, a fat, dignified, hard-working son-of-a-bitch, who regards Malcolm coolly.

Malcolm opens the meeting, "Greetings gentlemen. I come before the banking guild with humility."

Vice President Charleston, a reedy, uptight man dressed in a severe black suit sits to the President's right. He says, "Yes. Well. Lord Regent—I'm sorry, how are we to address you?"

Lord Regent Malcolm's tone is calm and slightly jovial, "Your Honor is the proper form of address."

The Vice President nods uncomfortably, "Your Honor, then. We have been meaning to meet with you this month. There are some things we'd like to discuss--"

He gets no further as Malcolm interrupts, "First, if I may, I have a proposition."

"A proposition?" asks the perplexed Vice President. "Erm.. What sort of proposition?"

"Well, as you know, I have founded a new nation."

"Yes, yes, everyone in town knows, Malcolm. Erm... Your Honor."

"Well," says Malcolm, the light from the tremendous windows manages to land just right to put a twinkle in his eye. "As you know, our economy is a growing one—unlike your country."

For a wonder, grudging chuckles sweep around the assembled bureaucrats.

Lord Regent Malcolm continues, "And the House of Lords have decided that we should establish a new currency."

"A new currency?" asks the Vice President.

Nodding, Malcolm continues, "Something rock solid. Something backed by good, hard, modern ingenuity!"

This is, of course, a most absurd notion. It is completely the sort of thing that Vice President

Charleston would reject outright under normal circumstances. "What are you talking about?"

Letting his smile grow just a little wider, Malcolm continues, "I'm talking about the sort of thing that makes nations great! I'm talking about making *our* country great! But I can't do it without you. I need your help. If we establish a currency that the people believe in, then the United States will have to publicly acknowledge us as a sovereign nation."

These aren't normal circumstances. The Board of Directors is desperate. In a last ditch effort to appear in control of the situation, Vice President Charleston moderates his voice, adopts the attitude of the seasoned loan officer, the kind of person who knows exactly what the answer to his question is. He asks, "What is your offer, then?"

Lord Regent Malcolm's smile disappears. He is all business. This is it. He lays it on the line, "First National Bank will be annexed and renamed the Royal Bank of the Commonwealth. The board of directors will not change except in that it is answerable to the Lord Regent. The Royal Bank of the Commonwealth will also serve as the Royal Mint, printing our currency, the Mallor, and minting its coins. Mr. President, you will be the overseer of our Royal Reserve Bank. It will be owned by the state, but run as you see fit. A Royal Oversight Committee will be established to make sure everything is copacetic—and to keep our taxpayers happy. Also, you will be in charge of establishing a Royal Revenue Service."

Thunderstruck, Vice President Charleston asks, "Is that all?"

Lord Regent Malcolm says, "No. There is just one more thing."

"What more could you possibly want from us?" asks the Vice President.

"Oaths of fealty, as so many others have already given. Just fealty, gentlemen. Oh, and to sweeten the deal, I shall issue an edict that all mortgages, with the exception of mine, Lord High Chancellor Howser and Duke Burke will have to be paid. I can't have the Royal Bank going bankrupt now, can I?"

Vice President Charleston opens his mouth to speak, but doesn't get a word out as the bank President summons all of his dignity and says quite calmly, "That is a compelling offer, Your Honor. And we shall give it our full consideration."

After a short recess, a vote is called to consider the offer. It goes eight for, one against. And thus, the First National Bank is annexed and becomes the Royal Bank of the Commonwealth.

Back at the White House:

"Mr. President," says a lackey for the Joint Chiefs. He is very nervous because he has unpleasant news to deliver.

"Yes, what is it? I'm very busy."

"Ah, the Joint Chiefs could not come to this morning's meeting because a situation has come up."

"Yes?" says the President, pulling his glasses off and tossing them on top of some papers.

"Well, it's about that new nation situation. It turns out, Mr. President that, well, they more than likely *do* actually have a nuclear warhead in their possession. And their borders are expanding every day."

The President rubs his eyes. "I never should have let this go so far. Where did this nuke come from?"

"There is an Air Force base near the town. On the base is a warehouse where we've stored some Cold War era warheads. Nobody's been in there for twenty years. We found the catalogue in a file cabinet in the basement of the Pentagon. We've matched up all the serial numbers and, sure enough. One of them is missing."

"Well, shit on a stick," says the President.

"On the plus side, Mr. President, we're not even sure if they work anymore. They're really old. It's possible that key components have degraded over time."

"Okay, if we take one out to the desert and blow it up, will it tell us if the one they have works?"

"There is no way to know without attempting to detonate more. The EPA won't like that."

"Hmmm... Well, try one out. If it blows, at least we'll know that it's possible that they can blow it up. If it doesn't work, then... well, there'll still be a doubt."

"Yes, Mr. President."

"And I think it's high time we get the National Guard on this. Send them to this 'Commonwealth' and set up a perimeter. Let's keep this thing from getting any bigger. Cut them off. Electricity, phone, internet, cable, food, everything. Let's cut them off from the outside world."

"Are you suggesting, Mr. President, that we lay siege to them?"

The President starts at this. Then his face becomes grim. He says, "Yes. I believe that is exactly what I'm suggesting."

"Very good, Mr. President."

"That should about do it," says Howser about a week after the siege started. He and Burke and Malcolm are hunched over an electric water pump. All utilities have been cut off by the military and so they are largely cut off from the rest of civilization. Their small nation is suffering from the most vicious of all trade embargoes. It's worse than Cuba since there's no way to appeal to any other nations. Like Canada, for instance, whom

Malcolm had been in talks with right up until the siege.

Howser adjusts the angle of the solar panels that he has rigged to the water pump. This and the array of batteries will keep the block in fresh water. There is one of these on every block now and the people of the Commonwealth are feeling particularly smug about it.

The people are feeling good, but Malcolm is worried. He scratches his chest where an electrode is measuring his heartbeat. Howser had rigged up a dead man's trigger for the Bomb. If Malcolm were ever to be assassinated, the Bomb would detonate.

He says to Howser, "How's that satellite uplink coming along? We got internet yet?"

"Don't know yet," says Howser. "I was going to head over there as soon as I was finished here. See what they've got rigged up. If we can get a comm. satellite on the line, I think we can upload our videos to the YouTube. Don't imagine we'll be short of hits neither. This thing was already a hit before they cut off the electricity. People will love to see the tanks outside of town."

"Burke," says Malcolm. "How are food rationing programs going?"

"All I got to say is, it's a good thing we annexed the grain silos. I'm worried though. Army might try and take 'em. Cut off our food supply."

"Is there someplace we can move the grain?"

"It's possible. We've got warehouses inside of town. They were a nuisance and an eyesore before the seige. Now they might just save our asses."

"Call Count Johnson and have him get his people hauling the grain to those warehouses. At least we won't be short of bread."

Howser pulls out his walkie and tunes it to the House of Lords channel and calls out for Count Johnson. "Hey Duke Howser, what's up?"

"Hey Count, can you get your cousins and the old Chevy and start hauling the grain from the silos to that warehouse in town?"

Malcolm tunes them out as he surveys his land. He has taken to wearing a coronet of sorts. Not gold, like in the olden days, but stainless steel. Harv over at the hardware store had tooled it. Set it with a chunk of granite cut and polished so it gleamed right above his forehead.

As they reach the end of the block, they climb in the back of Malcolm's jeep and he instructs his driver to head off toward downtown.

When they reach the radio station, Mickey the owner and operator of Mickey's Computers says, "We are online, Lord Regent. Commonwealthnation.org is up and running, streaming fifteen cameras twenty-four seven!"

"That is superb news," says Malcolm. "Tell the Technocracy that I have a keg of beer waiting for them as promised."

Just then, Malcolm is greeted by Agents Lister and Townsend who are waiting outside. They are stuck in the siege as much as anybody. Malcolm had had them disarmed as soon as he had learned who they were and their authority as intelligence experts from a foreign nation made them a serious national security threat. But Malcolm couldn't see the sense in locking them away. He only confiscated their phones and their guns. And they couldn't leave or they'd likely get shot, since he'd also taken their badges and their snappy suits.

"Agents, how's the war effort?"

"This is not a laughing matter...Malcolm."

Malcolm laughed at their refusal to give him an honorific. It was always very obvious that they were avoiding using it. Just the same, he said, "Someday, I'll convince you both that this is right for the Commonwealth and for America."

"That is not possible," says one of the agents crisply. "Neither of us has a whimsical bone in our bodies."

"Now that's just not true. Everyone's got the propensity for flights of fancy from time to time. Just look at my town. Capital city of a glorious new nation. All of these folks are in this 'cause they've got imagination."

"That imagination is going to get everyone killed. And that bomb of yours is likely going to be the source of it. That dead man's trigger of yours is made of cobbled wires and half a telephone. What if it fails?"

"National pollsters have said that 95% of Commonwealth citizens believe that the Bomb *and* the dead man's trigger are good. Five percent were undecided, but they'll come around. Now, we could stand out here and have the same damn discussion that we always have, or you folks could tell me if there is anything new that you'd like to cover that we haven't already been over a million times."

Agents Lister and Townsend look at each other. Then back at Malcolm. "The Army might be gearing up for an assault."

"Okay, A, how would you know that? And B, why the hell would they attack us? We have the Bomb."

"In answer to your first question, we have binoculars. As to the second, it appears they are calling your bluff."

"Get me the President!" shouts Malcolm.

It is tricky to get the President on the phone. It requires a delicate negotiation. It requires tact. It requires, as it turns out, getting Duke Howser's cousin Jake to walk toward the tanks with a white flag above his head. The difficulty arises when, as he approaches an entire armored brigade and a platoon of be-rifled teenagers, he does what any sane coward would do. He faints.

A squad of soldiers is deployed to recover the supposed defector. In a tent, about fifteen minutes later, he is revived through the use of smelling salts. An officer, a General, specifically General Jameson, US Army, stands over him. His breast is ornamented with a huge rectangle of tiny colored ribbons and an array of medallions jingles when he moves. He has one of those square jaws that you only see in the movies and wears mirrored sunglasses despite the gloom in the tent. His hat has four stars across the forehead. This guy's the real deal.

"Son, it's okay. You're back in America. It's a brave thing you've done."

"Wow," says Jake. "Yeah, I guess it is."

"Now, son, I know you've been through a lot. But the terms of your defection are as follows. You get a free pardon if you can tell me all about the town's defenses."

"Um... defection?"

"You're defecting to America, aren't you?"

"No, I've come to set up a meeting with the President."

General Jameson's face darkens. "You want to talk to the President?"

"No. The Lord Regent does."

The General raises his hand to deposit a stub of an unlit cigar in the corner of his mouth. He chews on it for a moment, pulls it back out with two gnarled fingers and spits a fleck of tobacco on the ground. He says, "You wait here, son. Keep a watch on him."

"Is this Malcolm?... Oh hell is this thing working? No... I think it's a bad connection."

"Hello? Mr. President?"

"Oh, I think I hear him. Yes? Hello? I think there's a delay."

"Well, you blew up our cellular tower."

"Yes, well. You declared war on us."

"I did no such thing. Ours was a peaceful secession."

"Oh hell, this thing is getting out of hand. Let's start over. Greetings, Lord Regent of the Commonwealth."

"Yes, greetings, Mr. President."

"Can I call you Malcolm?"

"Absolutely, Mr. President."

"Malcolm, I'm going to lay it on the line. Lord knows I don't need another war on my hands. America has more wars that we can handle right now. What do I need to do to get you to come back to us?"

"There is nothing you can do. My people are pretty determined to see this through."

"You have to realize that this is a losing battle. I mean, think of the children."

"I'm not the one laying seige on a tiny nation in the Midwest."

"Yes, but you are the one who seceded from the United States of America. I mean, how did you think this would go down?"

"Look, Mr. President, here's what I'll do for you. You withdraw all of your troops and open up trade negotiations and the Commonwealth will stop expanding her borders. We'll stop right where we are."

"You know I can't do that, Malcolm. If I let you secede without a fight, what's to stop others from seceding? This has to stop or it could undermine everything that America stands for."

"You must understand, Mr. President, that whatever it is that America does or does not stand for is no longer our concern. We are a young nation that is being beset by a larger, brutish power. How do you think this looks to the other nations? It's got to be bad P.R."

"How can you possibly expect me to withdraw our troops?"

"The way I see it, you don't have much of a choice."

"How do you figure?"

"Consider the possible outcomes of the siege. We currently have an active satellite linkup with a French satellite which is streaming live on the internet from every video camera in town. The whole world knows exactly what is going on. If you continue the siege and we run out of resources, my people will starve and it will be at your hands.

If you assault us, how do you think that will look? A large military invading a defenseless town."

"Defenseless? You have one of our nukes! And you can't expect me to believe that you are all unarmed."

"Compared to tanks and bombers we are. A few hundred hunting rifles are not going to stand up to that. And what good is one nuke. All I can do is blow us all to hell."

"So am I right in assuming you have no real intention of using that bomb of yours?"

"I have not ruled it out. I have the full support of my people if such a situation were to occur. And, as you are no doubt aware, I have been fitted with a dead man's trigger. We would rather die than be a part of your dysfunctional nation ever again."

"I see."

"Your move, Mr. President."

"Your bomb won't work, Malcolm."

"What makes you say that?"

"We tested one from the same lot. It malfunctioned."

"That proves nothing. You still can't be absolutely sure that I won't destroy your entire invading force should you attack. And they are not but children themselves."

"Malcolm, you can't be serious!"

"Mr. President, I am deadly serious. You have twenty-four hours to withdraw your troops or we will blow the Bomb."

"Malcolm, be reasonable."

"Twenty-four hours, Mr. President. Commonwealth out."

"That went well," says Duke Howser.

"You think so?" asks Malcolm. "I'd like to see 'em assault us now."

"Will you really blow it?" asks one of the special agents.

Malcolm looks around at all of the assembled lords and ladies in the high school cafeteria where the President of the United States had just met with Malcolm live via satellite. He addresses his people. "People of the Commonwealth. What say you? If they assault our city and all seems lost, should we surrender? Should we give up like cowards? Should we abandon the dream of an independent nation that we have strived for these many months?"

"NO!" comes the resounding cry from the crowd. They are waving the tiny Commonwealth flags that Mrs. Burke had been making around the clock. It is blue and white with a single golden star in the center. It is a little abstract for Malcolm's tastes, but the people really seem to rally behind it.

"Well, then what say you? Are you prepared to give up everything, even your lives to protect the seed of an idea that makes our nation great? Should I detonate the warhead if they invade our city? Should we take them with us and send a clear signal to all tyrant powers everywhere that their aggression will not go unpunished? I wish to call for a vote. If even a single dissenter is among you, I will not detonate the warhead. All in favor of ultimate sacrifice!"

"AYE!" comes the fervent cry from the crowd.

"All opposed!"

There is absolutely no way of knowing how many dissenters there were in the crowd. Damn near all six or so billion people on planet Earth have watched the video of the last moments of the Commonwealth. Medical professionals are in general agreement that the cause of death was a massive coronary embolism, or possibly an aneurism. A few have suggested a stroke, but, of course, the video ends abruptly after Malcolm's collapse. In the end, there's really no way to be sure.

The mushroom cloud was visible for miles around and there isn't a soul that saw it that didn't know what it meant. The President gave a speech. It was moving. It was heartfelt. It was bullshit, but that didn't matter. The point is, the President fucked up big time and everyone knew it. As with everything, nobody could ever say just exactly how the President could have handled it differently. He did not win his bid for reelection. You can't expect to keep your job when you allow a smallish rural community to blow itself to kingdom come.

The President's last act as President was to sign into law a bill that would require the dismantling of every stored nuclear warhead in the country. It is generally agreed that it is probably the best thing he did with his presidency.
As for the smoldering crater that was the Commonwealth, well, it is far too radioactive to support comfortable human life for several hundred years.

Angel Bob
By M.H. Kent

"Angel Bob" is a quirky story brought to us by M. H. Kent. He is an avid fan of British comedy in all forms and anything dealing with the end of civilization. In addition to his short stories he is also working on a novel and writing what he calls, a "neo-classical electronic symphony". We hope to one day know what that means.

Despite the generally negative press that being dead gets, Bob was finding it to be quite enjoyable. It had happened suddenly, a horrible and unusually fiery automobile accident, which hadn't allowed him any opportunity to say goodbye to certain loved ones or enjoy orange sherbet for the last time but all in all he was pleased with being deceased. After flames and significant blood loss had taken their toll on his mortal form, Bob awoke among a field of spring flowers stretching into eternity in a wash of blues and yellows. A swirling sky of violet and blue held thin ribbon clouds above him, the sight was dizzying yet he could not help but be transfixed by it all. Peace consumed every bit and piece of his being, flashes of life came to him like a sideshow but he disregarded them in favour of the brilliance overhead.

Bob lay among the buds of the afterlife with little care to the time that passed by, if in fact time had any meaning after death, it may have been days since he arrived but there was no way to tell. Just when the first meager thoughts entered his head that there must be more to the afterlife than this, a man appeared in the space above him and the great expanse of flowers faded away into the abyss.

"Bob," said the man with a ridiculously friendly smile. "You're dead."

"I know," said Bob.

"That's good. We wouldn't want any confusion. My name is Peter," he said and suddenly up became down, left became right and the two were sitting in a wood panelled office with a massive oak desk and floor to ceiling stained glass windows on the wall behind it.

"Jesus Christ!" Exclaimed Bob, shocked by the sudden transition. Turning around, Peter glanced at the stained glass and shook his head.

"No, that's just a picture of him. He's actually smaller in person," said Peter.

Bob adjusted himself in the overstuffed leather chair he now found himself sitting in and eyed the mini-bar at the side of the room. Peter stood and poured them each two fingers of what Bob could only assume was a well aged scotch then returned to his seat behind the desk.

"Well, as long as you're so well adjusted to the whole, 'being dead' thing," said Peter, "let's just get down to it then shall we? You've made it to heaven, good for you. After a review of your life, I've decided that you meet the requirements needed to enjoy a life of comfort and happiness here with us in heaven. There is one thing, a small thing really, nothing too big." Sipping his drink, which he had assumed correctly at being a finely aged scotch, Bob reclined in his chair.

"Sure, right, shoot," said Bob.

"You led a pretty good life, nothing of note that would get you on the heaven blacklist. We're quite happy to have you, despite your lifelong insistence that God, nor heaven, actually existed. Obviously if that had been a problem we wouldn't be having this conversation. We don't really care what you're general beliefs were in life, only whether or not you were a nice person, and you were. The downside, if you can really call it that, is that you'll be assigned a job to help out around here. You see, managing the cosmos is quite complicated and recently it's become even more so, to the point where we need the help of everyone to keep it all going as smoothly as possible." Peter explained, and then sipped his drink waiting for Bob's reply.

"A job?" asked Bob, who found the idea unexpected, as if heaven itself wasn't unexpected enough for him. It couldn't be all that bad, he thought, this was heaven after all. If this was indeed the land of comfort and happiness, they wouldn't be making him dig ditches or answer phones, if there were phones in heaven, he couldn't imagine there would be.

"Yes, a job." said Peter. "We've got you slated to take over a position in the soul distribution center, entry level of course, we find atheists to be too indecisive for management positions."

"Alright, when do I start?" asked Bob.

"Right away," said Peter with a grin and the room collapsed in on itself then disappeared.

***

"Mr. Jones?" asked a petite nurse in lavender scrubs as she leaned into the waiting room at Mercy General Hospital. Mr. Jones looked up from the fishing magazine that he had been attempting to read to take his mind off what seemed to be an eternity of waiting.

"Um, yes? I mean, yes, hello. How is it going? Is my wife going to be alright?" He said, leaping to his feet and tossing the magazine aside. The nurse smiled at his nervousness,

"It's alright, Mr. Jones, everything is going to be fine. I take it this is your first time?" she asked.

"Yes, first time," Mr. Jones said, blushing slightly.

"Well, you're going to be fine, you're wife is resting comfortably. You can see her now if you'd like. I'll take you to her."

"Thank you," said Mr. Jones and he followed the nurse down the corridor.

***

Bob flicked the little God bobble-head on his desk and smiled as it danced about with its content grin and intricately moulded white hair. Even as a lowly soul assignment officer, third class, he had a massive office with a fantastic view of a mountain stream that fed into a clear lake surrounded by majestic peaks. This was heaven after all.

"Right, let's assign some souls." He said, logging into his computer terminal. A welcoming cloud with a smiling face popped onto the screen and happily announced that he had two-thousand and seventy five souls waiting for assignment. This might be a bit harder than the instructor in training had made it out to be; he thought, then cracked his knuckles and dove right in. He started simple, matching older souls with potentially easy positions on Earth, younger souls with almost certain hardship to give them some experience, each according to the plan that was outlined in the morning's new hire orientation. This seemed simple enough, Bob thought to himself, picking up speed and humming a happy tune as he worked. Two hundred, three hundred, four hundred souls set for the future and it was still too early for his first coffee break. The names flew across his screen, his fingers blazed across the glossy white keys of his keyboard; the will of God was manifest in his keen matching skills. A soul sent to a new position in China, one to England, another to a remote village in Brazil. Twenty more with a whistle on his lips and the sun shone over the valley outside making a brilliant reflection on his mountain lake.

　　　　Bob pushed himself away from his desk with the satisfaction of a job well done and decided it was time for a coffee break. Out of his office and down the hall he found himself nearly skipping like a child, nearly a third of the way done with his list. He thought maybe he would get done early and could take a walk around his mountain lake to enjoy the afternoon. Just as he was pouring his coffee however, the intercom chimed to life with a cheerful voice.

"Angel Bob," it sang, "Angel Bob, soul assignment officer, third class, please report to supervisor Rhonda's office. Please report to supervisor Rhonda's office straight away, please."

Bob was certain they had noticed his amazing progress and were going to promote him to second class on his very first day. What else could it be about? Bob topped off his coffee then headed down to the end of the hallway to a massive wooden door intricately carved with cherubs, apples and adorable children. Knocking twice, the door opened by itself to reveal a dimly lit office with dark red walls and a dark mahogany desk where a thin brunette woman sat with a perplexed look across her tight features.

"Bob, sit down." She said sharply. Perching himself on a wooden stool, which was the only other piece of furniture in the room, Bob teetered patiently as she shuffled through a stack of papers.

"Bob, I'm Rhonda, your supervisor. How would you rate your performance this morning?" She asked.

"Fantastic." Bob said with a smile.

"Interesting," said Rhonda, "interesting. Having fun are we?" Bob thought about it a minute then replied cheerfully.

"Actually, yes. It's been really nice, thanks for asking." he said.

"Any problems? Questions about soul assignment?" She continued with the questions.

"Not that I can think of." said Bob, sipping his coffee.

"Well, if you're so adept at the job, then perhaps you can explain why you double booked a soul this morning?" She said, giving him a cold stare that froze him mid sip.

"I, um, what?" Bob muttered into the coffee cup.

"Double booking is a serious issue, it's only happened twice and never under my supervision. I would like to know how you made such a gross error. We take our duty very seriously here, its important work, work that must be done with the utmost diligence otherwise it can have grave effects on the world below. Do you take this seriously, Bob? Is this some sort of game to you?"

Bob sat unable to speak, this was the first time since he arrived that he felt unsettled by anything and he felt the contentment of eternal bliss draining out of him. He tried desperately to remember all the assignments he made that morning but there were too many, nothing had seemed out of the ordinary, he was sure that he done everything the way he was supposed to.

"Bob?" Rhonda asked, continuing the uncomfortable stare.

"Well, no, not at all." Bob said quietly in his defense.

"What do you think we should do about this, Bob? How would you suggest we go about fixing this problem?" Her questions were traps wrapped in puzzles, he was sure that he had done everything according to plan but here Rhonda sat giving him the worst cold stare he had ever experienced in this life or the previous. Where did he go wrong? How in heaven did he double book a soul? Bob furiously continued to pour over the hundreds of assignments he had made that morning then it hit him like a train.

"Twins," he whispered. They had made such a fuss about it during training, but he had been so transfixed by the sinfully good jelly doughnuts he had missed part of the instructions for dealing with twins. He immediately cursed his love for pastries as Rhonda stretched her hands across her desk and nodded slowly.

"Yes, Bob, twins. The Jones twins of Minneapolis, due in the morning and you've assigned them both the same soul. Apparently you missed the part during training that explained that twins show up as a single entry in the listings and that you must expand that entry to properly enter a soul for each one. This is a serious matter and I hope you appreciate the mess you've caused for everyone," said Rhonda.

"I'm sorry, I really am. I thought I was doing a good job. Can't we just use one of the souls that I haven't assigned yet? There must be thousands of souls just waiting for assignment. What about one of them?" he said, trying to think of a way to make this right. Rhonda shook her head and sighed. Bob squirmed on his stool that was becoming more and more uncomfortable as the conversation continued to become increasingly worse for him.

"It's not as simple as you would think, Bob. Twins require souls that are intertwined at the deepest level, souls that share such synchronicity of being that they are attuned to each other on levels that transcend the traditional sense of human interconnection, two souls that share such qualities that they may be considered to be identical to other than the most careful of observer. This, Bob, is the problem that we now face. You have already assigned them a soul and the ideal partner soul was tragically assigned to a small boy in India and those assignments cannot be undone! We cannot simply pull any soul from the list, the balance must be upheld." Rhonda ended her speech and sighed heavily. "There's only one thing we can do at this point. Only one person that can sort all of this out and makes things right again."

"Who?" asked Bob.

"God."

***

The hospital room exploded into panic, nurses frantically took vital signs and recorded them on clipboards. A doctor tied his apron while listening to the updates on Mrs. Jones' condition. Mr. Jones spun in circles trying to get an answer from anyone about what was going on with his wife but everyone was too busy to give him one. In the confusion, Mr. Jones found himself pushed out of the room and into the hallway where a sick feeling began to fill his stomach.

***

It is a lesser known fact that on the seventh day that God took to rest up from creating life, the universe and everything else, he used the time to design himself a cozy little getaway where he could be alone with his thoughts now that there were other people around to ask him about them. Especially in this busy time, with the cosmos continually expanding and so many souls to look after, he spent most of his time in this getaway so he could hide from the commotion and focus on the things that he truly enjoyed. Rarely was he consulted on the daily business of the universe, thousands of years of trial and error had produced a well oiled machine that nearly ran itself, everyone playing their parts as they had for millions of years.

Today though, God knew that something was wrong, he felt it deep in his bones and waited patiently for the trouble makers to come knocking on his door. He had been weaving and shaping the fabric of existence into a new galaxy that morning, his favourite thing to do, and had considered not bothering with the whole mess so he could continue to work on the problem of a creating a stable quadruple black hole system. Of course he had choirs of angels at his disposal to deal with issues of this sort but he liked to handle them personally from time to time to keep connected to his creations and ensure that everyone still knew he had the chops to run existence.

He knew they would knock just before lunchtime and settled himself into his favourite chair, a large, black leather number that really contrasted with his white robes giving him a dramatic appearance. In the past he would have used the over the top, 'voice from the clouds' bit, but ever since the Wizard of Oz the whole thing seemed a little silly. Now he opted for a more relaxed 'lounge' feel where he thought people could really open up to him, share their true feelings and maybe get to know him as more than just the supreme ruler of everything. The jury was still out on whether this approach was working however.

Two sharp raps on the door came just as he knew they would, he waved the door open and Rhonda and Bob stood in the doorway waiting to be invited inside.

"Come." said God, gesturing to a pair of comfortable looking chairs facing his own. Rhonda and Bob sat as instructed, Rhonda kept her eyes on her hands in her lap but Bob couldn't help but stare in amazement. Here he was the creator of it all sitting just feet away and beaming with light. Bob found himself wishing that the first time he met God wasn't due to the fact that he had made such a terrible error on his first day at work.

"Rhonda, Bob, very lovely to see you both. Of course I know why you both are here and I know that this must be taken care of as quickly as possible, but could I get either of you something to drink?" asked God, to which Rhonda politely shook her head but Bob raised a hand.

"I'd love a cup of coffee," said Bob. God waved his hand and a steaming cup of the most delicious cup of coffee Bob had ever had appeared in his hand, Bob took a sip and smiled, God smiled as well.

"I'm glad you like it, it's rare that anyone takes me up on my offers, they all act like they'd be putting me out by asking for a drink or a snack. I created the theory and practice of sustenance in a few hours but they act like making a simple cup of tea would be a hassle. A human trait that I'm not sure I'll ever understand. I do enjoy tea, wonderful stuff, partial to Earl Gray myself." said God, who created a small side table with a cup of tea upon it next to his chair and lifted the cup towards Bob. "Cheers."

"Cheers," replied Bob and they both sipped their beverages. Rhonda looked in amazement at the two of them, enjoying hot drinks together when there was a serious matter that required immediate attention.

"Yes, yes. Don't you fret, Rhonda," said God, setting his cup on the table and folding his hands in his lap. "I know you're concerned about the mistake that Bob made this morning regarding the souls for the Jones twins. It's a simple solution, one that I came up with before the two of you even came into this room, in fact right after the mistake had been made. All shall be made right, don't you worry Miss Rhonda." Rhonda forced herself to smile. One didn't have to be a deity to see that she felt Bob was getting off lightly.

"Of course sir, you are wise and I never had a doubt that you would have a prompt solution to this matter. I am simply wondering if we should reconsider Bob's current position as a soul assignment officer, third class." Rhonda said, gesturing to Bob who couldn't help smiling as he enjoyed the supreme superiority of his holy beverage. Raising a bushy white eyebrow, God looked Bob over carefully as if he was deep in thought, one of the many habits he had picked up from humans over the years. He found emulating their behaviours made them more comfortable when talking to them.

"Yes, indeed, I agree with you that this perhaps is not the position that Bob should have been assigned to, he lacks the attention to detail that one is required to have to properly attend to the assignment of souls." said God.

"I agree, sir," smiled Rhonda, happy that God shared her opinion of the situation.

***

Mr. Jones paced about the waiting room with volatile feelings of helplessness and impatience. The nurses had been nice enough to check up on him at the top of every hour, telling him not to worry but never telling him what exactly was going on so he could stop worrying. He wasn't a stupid man; he knew enough about the process that if anyone could just give him an idea he could put his mind to rest.

"That's it," he said, steeling himself with a deep breath and coming to the decision that he was going down to that room and demanding some sort of an answer. Before he could make it out of the room however, the doctor turned the corner with a smile beaming across his face.

"Mr. Jones?" The doctor asked.

"Yes?" He said, his stress melting away upon seeing the doctor's happy face.

"Your wife is fine and we were able to save both of the babies. You can come in now if you'd like."

"Thank you, thank you so much doctor." Mr. Jones nearly erupted in tears of joy and followed the doctor down the hall to the room where his wife lay, tired but happy to be holding their bundled twins.

"Sam!" She cried.

"Emily!" Mr. Jones shouted and ran to her bedside, wiping away the sweat from her brow and kissing her gently on the forehead. "Are you alright? Is everything okay?"

"Of course, Sam, we're doing fine." Mrs. Jones smiled. "They want to know what names to put on the birth certificate. You never told me what you had decided."

"Right, of course." He looked over his children lovingly, studying their tiny features with care. "Well, we of course had decided to name one after your grandmother, Elizabeth. Elizabeth Anne Jones is your name little one." He said, gently touching the squirming newborn at Mrs. Jones left side.

"And?" asked Mrs. Jones.

"I was in the waiting room and it just came to me, not sure why, but I really like it." He said.

"It's alright, whatever you decide, dear." Mrs. Jones smiled. Mr. Jones leaned over and carefully shook the other child's tiny hand.

"Good to finally meet you, Rhonda."

* * *

Meanwhile in heaven, Bob gave God a confused glance to which God simply replied. "I never cared much for her." He said, to which Bob raised his mug.

Son of Storms
By Melvin Shem

*Melvin Shem is a creative writer from northern
Minnesota who brings us "Son of Storms". He
began crafting stories in grade school and now
passes his love for literature onto his students as a
teacher of creative writing. In his free time he
enjoys gardening, French films and practicing the
ancient art of Ken-do.*

The forest around the council was still, a
testimony to the seriousness of the matter that was
being discussed. The Pointed Ones did not meet in
high councils like this often, but when they did each
of the 12 main forests of the Green Ring were
represented.

They were fair of form, the Pointed Ones,
calm of face and slow to anger. When normally this
council met, the august few often had to discuss
something to do with the growth of the Forests. Be
it a disease of the trees, or a conflagration of the
flowers, the councils had been as placid as a frozen
pond. Tonight it was different; this was the first in
remembered history to be called to deal with the
incursions of the Out Kingdoms.

A younger Pointed One stepped into the
center of the ring. "We must fight this time! The
forests are losing their equilibrium, and cannot
stand much more of the outlanders harvests!"

The rest of the circle scowled at him, this
Sorden Frestor, the youngest of the council. They'd

not have met with him at all, but he had enough respect in his home forest to represent them here.

Another spoke from his seat, without moving to the center. "We cannot fight. Some have tried, and died from their own forests rejecting them before they could make an attack. We are made as farmers, and tenders of the land. Fighting is impossible for us."

"Please, this talk of fighting sickens me, and is perhaps as distasteful to the others. Will anyone else speak?" This was Worden Frestor, guardian of an elder forest on the far side of the ring, also the one whose forest was least in danger from the outlanders.

The youngest retook his seat. Another took his place in the center. "Perhaps we can weather this as we weather the twin storms, Taxim and Loftil? We must be like the trees and plants of the forest when the twin gods of destruction come...we must bend and sway."

This caused some upset among the members, Sorden Frestor the loudest. "These are not the twin Storms!"

"They do not just destroy the woods, they consume!"

"They have no plans at all, they just take and use, take and use!" Another said, hands flailing about in the light of the moon.

"What shall we do?"

The hours passed, with more discussion, but no course of action that all could agree on. Finally Worden Frestor spoke again. "I see no solution here. Perhaps it would be best to break now, and meet when again the sun is longest in the sky."

Sorden Frestor stamped the ground in anger. "My forest, by then, will have died, and all the Pointed Ones that I represent with it!"

It appeared that another disorderly outburst was likely from all the members. It was then that a word broke out in the quiet. "Wait."

It came from one whom had said nothing in the last hours, but sat and scratched in the dirt with his walking stick. All attention turned to him, but he remained silent for some time. All that could be heard was the scratching of the stick. He spoke again, breaking the silence.

"It seems to me, as our nature prevents us from fighting, and such action would be needed, that we need help from one among those-who-eat-meat."

"What good is this? They all work for the same kingdoms that are pillaging our homes!" An elder across the circle shouted.

"Yes, and if they fight each other, the blood shall stain the land, and angry blood is poison! This plan does us no good!" Sorden Frestor shouted.

The dirt sketcher allowed these arguments and others to pass over him, while he continued dragging the point of his stick over the ground. As the others quieted, he looked up, his eyes glowing in the moonlight. "I did not say it would be help from those who rape our forests. I speak of another, from another ring."

"Who? Who is this saviour? It will take too long, regardless. Any who leave the forests shall die from the removal," Sorden Frestor was angry, and the volume in his voice rose with each word, "How will this idea help, I ask again?"

The dirt sketcher looked through the youngest. "Listen to the words of Norden Frestor, all of you: the one I speak of is Onweer Racolga."

Worden Frestor, a woman of some standing, asked, "Who is this Onweer Racolga? Can anyone share the growth of this being?"

The Pointed One across from her stood up and spoke. "The migrating animals tell tales of him. They say as one of the preeminent shamans of the desert ring he destroyed some of the mating grounds."

Another spoke. "The kingdom dwellers speak of him as well. It is said that on the distant ring his name is feared more than death, for he can destroy not only an individual, but the entire tribe and land that they work."

"It is said that he is the son of the twin storms."

"Bah. That is said of every shaman of the sand. How are we to find this saviour and if we do, how will a mere storm he calls be able to help?" Sorden Frestor spoke.

Norden Frestor spoke again, "Anyone who can drive off our guardians, they-who-rip-arms, they-who-fear-nothing, will be able to stop the outlanders."

"How do you know that he can do these things?"

"Onweer Racolga dwells within my domain. He can go where we and our familiars dare not, and for the peace from the hunters that I may offer him, he may help us."

"Is there no cost other than this?" Worden Frestor asked.

"There is always unforeseen cost in any action, as we all have experienced, though Sorden Frestor perhaps least of all. But it seems to me when the extinction of one of our own is called in question, and more to follow, we must pay the costs – known and unknown," Norden Frestor stood up.

All of the Pointed Ones were quiet. "Very well, Norden Frestor, as we can find no reason not to try this course, you have the council's permission to meet with Onweer Racolga and enlist his help. May the peace of the forest be upon you."

It was a week later when Norden Frestor encountered Onweer Racolga. The Pointed One followed the fear scent that they-who-fear-nothing left. This fear was rare, and because of this, the trail was strong and easy to follow. Norden Frestor came upon the cave where the shaman dwelt, hidden in the black and back ways of his forest.

"Onweer Racolga. By the power of my forest, I summon you." Norden Frestor stood, leaning upon his walking stick.

Onweer Racolga stepped out. He was a short man, skin wrapped tightly about the bones that jutted out due to small diet. He was wrapped in white cloths, stained by his time among the forest. His face was tight, eyes slit from long years on the desert sand, and beard spotted with gray. He stared at the Pointed One.

"What in the name of the twin storms are you?" He asked.

"I am Norden Frestor, highest ranked among my people in this forest. We have a favor to ask of you, Onweer Racolga," Norden Frestor nodded towards him.

"I don't grant favors." The man turned to walk back into his cave.

"We can grant you peace in this forest, shaman," Norden Frestor spoke, "We can give you the peace of the woodlands, such a gift has never before been offered to one of your kind."

"The peace of the forest?" Onweer's eyes glinted, "What good will that do to me? Your creatures who haunt me offer enough distraction to keep me busy for some time. I have no need of peace."

"Then why run from your sands, desert walker?" The Pointed One asked, "Does not your soul seek peace? Perhaps the peace of death?"

Onweer turned from walking away, hands clenching his robes. "Is that a threat?"

"Merely an observation."

"No thing can grant me the peace I seek."

"The forest, if time enough is spent here, can. It can even give salve enough to one who destroyed his entire clan in the fit of his stormcalling."

"So you've heard of that, have you? I tell you, it wasn't my intention, but once raiders have called havoc there is no stopping them," Onweer Racolga shrugged, then snarled, "But what should that matter to you, in these paradises that know no bandit?"

"Are you trying to convince me of your observations, or yourself?"

Onweer Racolga said nothing, but sat in front of the Pointed One. "Norden Frestor. You see many things, and offer me something that cannot easily be won. What is the price?"

Norden Frestor also sat down. He circled their heads with his stick as he spoke. "The Pointed Ones, the name that at first was given us by the outlanders but what we have now claimed as our own, are in danger. The Kingdoms pillage our forests, rape our land, and if not stopped will destroy us. We cannot fight them. We require your power."

"You want storms called down upon them?"

"Not just any storms, Onweer Racolga. The passages of the twin storms Taxim and Loftil barely slow them down. It is said that you are the son of these two."

Onweer whispered, "No. I will not do it."

"We need the power of the twin storms, at once. You alone, it is said, are the one who can call both at once, in a blazing ring of power. The clans whisper of this, of the fearsome power you hold. It is told in the movements of the waves on the shores that echo through the rivers to the forests. We know that this has happened more than once, Onweer Racolga. You must do it again."

"You don't understand. Each time, I destroyed some part of myself. The storms once bidden are not heedful of any controls that shamans usually have. They are too powerful, and could easily destroy everything on this ring."

"There is a cost to any action, and you may blame us fully for anything that happens by our request. We will offer you the peace of the forest, and in time that will overcome your pain, and overcome what effects of this action are. We call the twin storms to witness that we Pointed Ones are the culpable parties," a breeze shifted at this last promise, a sign that the storms accepted the surety. Calm followed.

"That is our offer," Norden Frestor fell silent as the other considered.

"Will you not heed my warning? The cost is too high, Pointed One. Would you sacrifice this forest in order to save it? That is what you are asking me to do, and it is not even mine to sacrifice," Onweer Racolga looked out into the woods.

"Our council has decided. We have deliberated, and it is to you who we turn for our hope. I will leave you now to decide. We will know by your actions. If you take our offer, you have no need to fear anything in this forest again." Norden Frestor stood, took his stick and hobbled off into the forest, leaving no sign of his appearance or any leaf to shudder in his passing.

Never among the three rings had such a sight been seen. The twin storms converged at the same time on the Out Kingdoms of the forest ring, called by Onweer Racolga. The kingdoms were ripped to shreds instantly, the lightning of the one storm combining with the driving wind and rain from the other caused castles to fall, houses to burn, and weapons to fly through the air knowing no fealty to wielder or victim. The kingdoms were torn asunder.

The storms were angry this time, for the destruction seemed more than just random. If it was with their rumored son that they were angry with, they did still his bidding. The destruction was as Onweer Racolga had predicted: it was far greater in scope than the Pointed Ones had hoped. Perhaps in his quest for peace, Onweer Racolga called the storms with such conviction that the storms wished to destroy both sides of the conflict. Perhaps the shaman lost control of his powers. Perhaps the twin storms punished the Pointed Ones for failing to understand the terrible cost of storm shamans.

Fully half of the twelve main forests stood desolated, no leaf lying upon leaf, and the rivers mucked with the bodies of the animals among the detritus of the plants.

The storms, Taxim and Loftil, may have been godlings as the races believed. This time perhaps, they were angry with the pitiful creatures that called them down outside of their normal cycles. For after he summoned them, it seemed that Onweer Racolga was called up to the very center of their meeting, for he was never seen nor heard from again in the three rings.

That, at least, is one rumor of the fate of the shaman. It is also said that in his summoning he destroyed what was left of his humanity. It is claimed he became a storm unto himself. Suffice to say, he was no longer within the forest or the desert.

The additional price to be paid by the council came in the form of localized storms above the forest ring. It is said that three of the original council remained, Norden, Sodern and Worden Frestor, and that all three quaked at these storms that came upon them that were fierce in intensity and random in appearance.

These storms came to be known as the Onweer Racolga. And they seem to target only the forest ring of all three, and cannot be summoned by the shamans of the sand. In truth, none know the fate of Onweer Racolga, son of storms, and whether he found the peace he sought.

Constant
By Carrie Scifres

Carrie Scifres is a twenty-something Bemidji State alumni currently working on her second degree. Eventually she will be a librarian, constantly breaking her own imposed silence. She is an avid reader which she believes helps her writing.

I always thought, "Things will be different when I go to college;" a childhood spent untangling a cluster-fucked family tree of unpredictability will be replaced with a seasoned adult who oozes responsibility and stability. Got to love that optimism.

But first I had to learn independence, which as any freshmen knows is never achieved gracefully in college. So I faltered and failed in a spectacular fashion: I couldn't get to class, my grades slipped and I eventually withdrew from college. After tears and tantrums galore, I realized that my problems were bigger than I could manage; they were more extensive than most college freshmen's. When I realized that my dreams were being swallowed by my failures, I made things worse by becoming suicidal and, eventually, hospitalized. The diagnoses, therapists and medications followed close behind.

Eventually I clawed my way back onto the path that I dreamed of. It had its bumps - three hospital stints and a year and half in a halfway home - but I tried not to falter from my chosen trail of a college degree and a well balanced life. I willed my happily-ever-after with its own white picket fence. I returned to college aware that I had to release some of my hopes - like being the best student – in order to hold onto my dream.

I strove for independence. But when my adulthood was christened with restrictions and failures I became stunted in the ways of "normal" life. All of my happy, carefree and careless actions, like hopping a Greyhound and seeing the world, turned into frightening journeys which would leave me confronting each decision. I was told such actions were symptoms of bi-polar disorder. But I had my close circle of friends who knew who I was even when I questioned it. Slowly, I rebuilt my adventurous side into a safe, well-planned school adventure.

There were requirements that only I had to meet, but I joyfully crawled over their hurdles and hesitations. I was going to experience London, Paris and Rome, places where the world's true Romantics lived. I was ready for the experiences that would help me build into the woman my childhood self would be proud of.

I had known who he was for most of my childhood, and I had always thought he was cute.
We were both crashing at a friend's house.
I would leave for England in five days.
My friends threw a party.
I took my medication to get some sleep.
It came in flashes;
I remember him asking if anyone had any condoms.
I was in a tar filled bog and couldn't break free to shout NO!

In fear and trepidation,
hiding in the basement,
* realizing he was waiting for me.*
I tried to struggle but he held me down.
Frightened and chilled to my soul,
* I huddled on the floor trying to curl into the*
smallest ball.
A loss of the last measure of trust and innocence
vanished in one slow medicated blink of my eyes.

The physical ramifications of the rape were the easiest to overcome. A little tearing and more medication, nothing I couldn't handle. Not surprisingly, it was the experience that I had to recover from.

I have impressions of the doctors, nurses and police officers that were present for my living nightmare but no clear picture of them. The attending nurse wavered between indifference at my experience, annoyance at my discomfort, and rudeness when she learned that all my hours of watching "Law and Order" had proven useless when faced with my own assault, which resulted in a failure to preserve evidence on my part.

After the invasive exams that achieved their supposed goal of stripping me of any respect I thought I had left, I was escorted to a large, startlingly sterile white room where I was faced with a new form of dissection; one of the soul instead of the physical self. The police officer was kind but silent when I relayed what fragmented moments I remembered. Raw and exposed, I felt judged. The worse was that I didn't remember all of it. Did I encourage? How much did I fight back? Am I really a victim if I don't remember?

I refused to give up the trip. I wouldn't let him take that too. First, I had to go to a *safe* place until we left; which meant I went back into in-treatment; my punishment for being a victim.

The trip proved to be a self-induced nightmare. It was meant to expand my narrow world; instead it tainted London, Paris and Rome forever. I wasn't allowed to talk about what happened; it might upset the other students. So I suffered silently. I continued to take the medications that facilitated my assault; it was a requirement. Each night I repeated the actions that took place that night.

Already I was an outsider, who wasn't allowed to drink or engage in the other students' social actives, which made it difficult to make those connections that I longed for. I couldn't wander along those withered streets because I feared their shadows.

Now, five years later it's as if I continued to clinch my eyes closed throughout the aftermath.

I force myself to say the word in conversation.

Rape.

I am stronger than a word. I talk about it as if it happened to someone else. Each time I forced it from my lips my body tenses in anticipation of the pain. The first time I said it I was frozen from reaction; a campaign between my body and my mind to stave off what my fragile state could not combat. But with each carefully placed off-hand omission, tiny prickles of raw searing pain traveled along my self-consciousness, imprinting an invisible tattoo; a steady piercing of pain and grief honoring my experience. I try to only allow it access to the surface depths, not yet ready to melt the part of me where my romantic girlhood images of my first time are held. I'm not ready for her heart to be broken too.

I've gone from the rape encompassing my every waking and sleeping thought, to it being a fleeting awareness that makes every muscle quiver in terror at random moments of my life; the grocery store when I spot a man that looks like him, when Europe is mentioned—guilty by association—or when a man touches me.

It makes me uncomfortable; it might be making you uncomfortable right now. You know it happens, but you selfishly want it to happen to someone you don't know. We've moved past blaming the victim but are still unsure of how to face the survivor. Shame and guilt consume you, caused by your relief that it wasn't you or someone you love.

I filled my medication today. That, like my new awareness, is a constant.

If you enjoyed these stories, please visit
www.theprojectmag.com
For more information about ordering the book,
background information on the process, upcoming
issues, polls to show author support, and how to
submit!

If you have any questions or concerns, please
contact us at submissions@theprojectmag.com